Praise for **The Secret of Grim Hill**, the first book of the "Grim Hill" series:

"... solid tween appeal ..." – *The Globe and Mail*

"... a protagonist who is self-centred enough to be interesting, a precocious kid sister who deserves her own book and a plot that bubbles along at a magical pace ... creepy enough to cast a spell over anyone who reads it!"
– *Resource Links*

"Cat is an engaging heroine, and Grimoire has just the right amount of evil ..."
– *January Magazine*

The Secret of Grim Hill

written by
Linda DeMeulemeester

Winner, Ontario Library Association Silver Birch Award

Selected, Canadian Toy Testing Council's "Great Books for Children"

Uncover the secrets that started it all ...
The Secret of Grim Hill
978-1-897073-53-7

Visit the official "**Grim Hill**" series website:
www.grimhill.com

Grim Hill
The Secret Deepens

Published by Lobster Press™
1620 Sherbrooke Street West, Suites C & D
Montréal, Québec H3H 1C9
Tel. (514) 904-1100 • Fax (514) 904-1101 • www.lobsterpress.com

Publisher: Alison Fripp
Editor: Meghan Nolan
Editorial Assistants: Emma Stephen and Brynn Smith-Raska
Proofreader: Mahak Jain
Cover Illustration: John Shroades
Graphic Design & Production: Tammy Desnoyers

We acknowledge the financial support of the Government of Canada
through the Book Publishing Industry Development Program (BPIDP)
for our publishing activities.

We acknowledge the support of the Canada
Council for the Arts for our publishing program.

The Canada Council | Le Conseil des Arts
for the Arts | du Canada

Library and Archives Canada Cataloguing in Publication

DeMeulemeester, Linda, 1956-
    Grim Hill : the secret deepens / written by Linda DeMeulemeester.

ISBN 978-1-897073-97-1

    1. Magic--Juvenile fiction. 2. Fairies--Juvenile fiction.
3. Sisters--Juvenile fiction. 4. Schools--Juvenile fiction.
5. Rescues--Juvenile fiction. I. Title.

PS8607.E58G75 2008   jC813'.6   C2008-901708-0

Google is a trademark of Google, Inc.; **Monopoly** is a trademark of Hasbro, Inc.

Printed and bound in Canada.

Text is printed on Rolland Enviro 100 Book,
100% recycled post-consumer fibre.

For my mother, Madelene Gill,
and in memory of my father, Allan Keith Page.

Acknowledgements: Enormous gratitude to Meghan Nolan for her
editorial direction. Thank you to John Shroades for another snazzy
cover, to Sean O'Beachain for the Celtic translations and pronuncia-
tions, and to Helix for perusing the early chapters. Much appreciation
to John for making sure I have time enough to write and to Alec and
Joey for not complaining about it. Many thanks to Janine Cross, a
good friend and a great writer who always has my back.

– Linda DeMeulemeester

Grim Hill
The Secret Deepens

written by
Linda DeMeulemeester

Lobster Press ™

CHAPTER 1

The Battle Begins

IT WAS A stupid argument, one better not to get involved in – except the new boy at school made my blood boil.

I leaned forward, but that only made Clive tower over me. So instead I drew myself up and put my hands on my hips. In my most menacing voice, I said, "What do you mean boys are better at soccer."

"Girls are better at other things. Like, well, not sports, but you know ..." Clive said in an arrogant way. When I turned to shut my locker and leave, he continued. "Guys are faster, stronger ... more agile. Sorry," he said with a smirk, "but you can't argue with nature."

"That's ... that's ... just crap." Okay, maybe that wasn't the cleverest reply, but it's difficult to think of smart remarks when your blood is pumping so hard behind your eyes that you see spots. Besides, I didn't like the way the sunlight came through the narrow hall window and pooled directly behind Clive. His black curly hair lit up like a halo, and his skin seemed to glow. Clive appeared as if he truly was a golden boy.

"'Crap' ... uh huh ... that's telling him, Cat." My friend Mia winced, twisting a strand of red hair around her finger. I didn't notice her coming up with anything better.

"Nothing personal," said Zach, the most popular boy in our grade. Once I had thought he liked me – that is, until I found out he had only liked me because he'd fallen under a spell. Actually last month the whole town had been under the magical glamour of fairies – fairies that were up to nothing but nasty things.

Zach put his hand against my locker door and swung it back and forth. "It's just that Darkmont High only has enough money in the budget to sponsor one soccer team and pay for the transportation and tournament costs. They are going to send their best team to the intramurals. That's us." Then he slammed my door shut with a clang to drive his point home.

He gave me that half-grin that should have made my heart beat faster, but it didn't. I wouldn't let it. Why did the guys think they were so great? I couldn't understand why Zach agreed with this new boy. He had seen the girls play and he knew how good we were.

"Who says you're the best team," I muttered. Even though the girls had formed our own team only a few weeks ago, our skills were awesome. Every single girl on the team had been in the Halloween match – the game most of us hardly remembered, and those of us who did, tried to forget how close we came to a terrible fate. But one thing was sure – we didn't forget all the skills we'd learned after hundreds of hours of soccer practice.

"Yeah," Amarjeet joined in the argument. "We can out-play you guys any day of the week."

"Right." Clive rolled his eyes and all the boys laughed.

How did Clive get to be so popular so fast? He'd only started Darkmont a couple of weeks before and already he was the captain of the soccer team. He acted so sure of himself, and even some of the girls standing around us smiled at him while he mocked us. It didn't help my opinion of him that I'd gotten off to such a rough start. I'd been the new kid in September, and any friend I had in the eighth grade was hard earned – even though I was popular in my old town. Besides, nobody had made me captain of the girls' team, and that was something I wanted more than anything.

I got an idea. "So you guys think your team's the best? Prove it."

The boys stopped laughing. Clive did a double take and asked, "What do you mean?"

"We'll have a soccer match – girls against the boys. Whoever wins gets to sign up as Darkmont's team for the intramurals."

"But you'll need a sponsor." Zach wasn't grinning anymore. Was he looking a little worried, perhaps?

"We'll get a sponsor." Amarjeet sounded as if she thought this was a great idea.

"Who?" asked Mitch, one of the school's best athletes. "It has to be a teacher." He ran his hand through the short stubble on his scalp. I couldn't help notice Mia watch his every move. I guess I wasn't the only one who missed the magical popularity we'd gained during the Halloween match.

Amarjeet shrugged her shoulders. Finding another teacher to sponsor us at Darkmont was as likely as kicking a ball and landing a goal two soccer fields away – while blindfolded. Teachers at Darkmont never seemed to have time to supervise extracurricular activities.

The bell rang and we scrambled to get to science class. Mia and I raced up the stairs along the dingy hallway with its yellowing linoleum and flickering lights. Mitch followed, nattering behind us. "Your girls' team doesn't have a chance. Don't you know all the top athletes in the world are men?"

As we walked into the classroom, I'd had about enough and shouted, "That's a load of crap!"

11

Mia rolled her eyes. I think she wished I'd expand my vocabulary. Worse, Ms. Dreeble had been writing on the board, and as her hand slid down, the black marker left a trail. She twisted around.

"Cat Peters, I beg your pardon. What kind of language is that?"

I meant to say "sorry" in a sincere way, but my temper flared. "The boys are saying that they deserve to be the soccer team Darkmont sponsors in the intramurals and that girls can't be the best athletes." And because it felt good to let this all out, I kept going. "It shouldn't be a given. All we want is a chance to prove it to them with a soccer match."

Ms. Dreeble peered over her glasses and said, "Come again? What's this all about?"

For once I made a wise choice and I didn't keep arguing. I told myself I should keep this whole silence thing in mind for future problems. "Ask Mitch," I said as innocently as possible. Then I quietly slipped away.

As Mitch and Ms. Dreeble got into it, I slid onto the lab stool wedged between Mia and Amanda. The classroom was super-crowded, but now it felt quite comfortable as I listened to Mitch seal his doom by saying, "But aren't there are a lot more famous male scientists?"

Science had never gone better. For the whole lab, Ms. Dreeble kept Mitch standing beside her desk as she recited a long list of female scientists. I ignored the lecture notes on the board about electrical charges. It seemed more important to scribble in my notebook as Ms. Dreeble rattled off famous women's names.

Mitch paled as he heard about Annie J. Cannon, an early astronomer, or Sophie Germain, who discovered an equation almost three hundred years ago that was still used in constructing today's skyscrapers. Most of what Ms. Dreeble was saying was news to me. That got me going even more.

Ms. Dreeble told the class that many of those scientists couldn't even publish their work under their own names because they were women. I swear, I could see a tear in her eye. It was all I could do not to stick my tongue out at Mitch. I'll admit I looked kind of smug.

When the bell rang and Mia and I filed out, Ms. Dreeble said, "Cat, Mia, please come see me."

I should have known she'd finally gotten around to me. I thought she forgot about my inappropriate language. Nervously, we walked back. First Ms. Dreeble frowned, and I began calculating how I'd pick up my little sister from school *and* serve detention. Then she said, "I'll be happy to sponsor the girls' soccer team."

I stood there with my mouth open, mostly because what was going through my mind was that I always felt as if she unfairly picked on me. Finally, I managed to chime in with Mia. "Wow, thank you ... that's ... great."

Then Mia and I rushed off to the cafeteria to tell Amarjeet and the other girls the good news. I was so impressed with Ms. Dreeble that I vowed to play the best soccer anyone had ever seen. Maybe I would even pay more attention in science.

Smells of onions and grease hit me as I entered the lunchroom. Darkmont wasn't exactly known for its gourmet cuisine. We circled the tables and told everyone about our sponsor. Mitch was updating the guys. I noticed a lot of the popular boys and girls sitting at his table, and when Clive's clear laughter rang around the room, I could guess what he thought was so amusing – that the girls weren't going to give him any competition. I got up and walked toward their table, determined to tell Clive just how wrong he was, but I lost some confidence when I spotted Emily sitting next to him.

Sure, Emily was a popular girl, but I'd come to think of her as one of us – meaning the group of girls who'd pulled together and fought the fairies on Grim Hill. We'd all worked together then. Besides, Emily was our team captain. How could she be such a sell-out sitting with the guys?

"As Mitch told you, Ms. Dreeble is sponsoring our team," I said to Clive. "Guess you're worried now."

"We're all good," said Clive glancing over his shoulder as the boys nodded in agreement. "We'll keep our end of the bargain. Whoever wins the match becomes the team Darkmont sponsors for the intramurals."

Then he held out his hand for me to shake. As if. But Mia came up behind me and whispered, "No point in being a bad sport." Was she falling under his charms as well? Even though I knew she had a point, I smiled when I said to him, "Let's hold off and shake hands on the soccer field when the girls are the winning team."

Then Emily stood up and crossed over to my side. She didn't seem the least bit angry. She giggled as she said to the boys, "We are going to mop you guys up on the soccer field. Cat's an awesome player, and so are Mia and Amarjeet."

"I'm sure they are. And I know you all play well," said Clive. Then he added with a grin, "For girls."

Everyone started to laugh. What was so funny? Didn't they see through this jerk? Didn't they know it wasn't just a game at stake? That we had to prove ourselves to these boys once and for all? I couldn't help but look around at everyone and shake my head.

"What's the matter, Cat?" Emily said. "It's all in fun,

right?"

"Right," I lied. I managed a nod. There was nothing that I wanted more than to score the winning goal. And only then would I walk up to Clive and say with a little smile, "Good game." Only then would we shake hands. I let that scene play over in my mind for most of the afternoon as I thought about how unfair things were sometimes.

Later in history class when Mr. Morrows discussed important inventions in the Industrial Revolution, I stuck my hand up.

"Yes, Cat?" Mr. Morrows looked kind of surprised. "*You* have a comment?"

Yes, I did – even though I usually tried to hide behind my textbook. "Ada Lovelace, the daughter of Lord Byron, invented the first software for the 'difference engine,' the great grandfather of the computer," I said checking my notes from Ms. Dreeble's lecture.

"That was late 1800s," said Clive who always stuck his hand up, "which wasn't the time of the Industrial Revolution."

"Um ... that's correct, Clive," said Mr. Morrows. Oh yeah, Clive always had the right answer, too. I seethed.

"Okay," I said. "Um ..." I scanned the notes. "Well how abut Caroline Herschel who helped discover Saturn's rings in the late 1700s."

"The right time, but that's not exactly an invention," Clive said in such a pompous way. "Besides, those women were only assistants or daughters of famous people."

I began ranting. "So what?" I said, but Mr. Morrows interrupted.

"Let's not get too sidetracked." Mr. Morrow's mustache twitched as if he was hiding a smile. What was so funny?

He cleared his throat. "And science is a collaborative field, Clive."

I wasn't exactly sure what that meant. Before I could decide if Mr. Morrows was on my side, he sprang a pop quiz. It only made me a lot angrier when Clive got the highest mark in the class, beating my own score by five marks. Who cared about steam engines anyway?

All the way home I imagined soccer plays while I dribbled every rock I could find and shot stones off my foot, pretending to score a goal. I had to beat Clive's ... uh ... the boys' team. As I turned down my street, I looked up at Grim Hill. It was all forest now, with no spooky school or soccer fields left. Instead, a green hill sat under a gray November sky, safe as could be ...

Except, no one ever walked up the hill anymore. No one. And right now, when I looked very carefully at the evergreen trees near the top of the hill, I thought I could see strange green and yellow lights flickering between them. I quickly looked away.

This is what it must feel like to be a villager looking up every day at the island volcano and wondering if it was going to erupt.

There were wicked fairies locked up inside that hill.

CHAPTER 2

A Sucker Trick

"**WHAT DO GIRLS** like?" asked Jasper.

It was the next day, and I wasn't really paying attention to my friend. We were strolling along the main street of our town. Jasper had finished his paper route, and we were killing time while I waited for my sister's swimming lessons to finish. It was parent/teacher night at our school, and my mom, who recently started a job as a secretary at Darkmont, had to work late.

The problem was that I was feeling a bit ashamed of myself, thinking I was making a big deal out of nothing the day before. So what if the boys were saying they were better? Basically we – the girls – were saying the same thing to them – that we'd beat them at the soccer match. Emily was right – it was all in fun, and at least for the next little while, we could all play soccer. I would be a good sport. I had to stop letting my temper get the best of me.

When Jasper repeated the question, "Really, what is it girls like?" I apologized and tried to think.

"Hmm ... what do girls like? That's easy," I said. "Bubble bath in plastic containers shaped like ice cream sundaes, tiny bottles with flowery smelling perfume, and cut-out dolls with lots of outfits, oh ... and fuzzy slippers that look like bunny rabbits."

Jasper shook his head and said, "That doesn't sound much like you, Cat." He got an odd look on his face and pushed his glasses up on his forehead until they rested on his spiked hair. Then he blushed a bit. "Or Mia for that matter."

I slid to a stop. "Weren't you asking for hints about what to get Sookie for her birthday?" My kid sister loved girly stuff, especially "older-girl" items made for littler kids – things like cherry-flavored lip gloss and purses that looked like kittens or puppies. I was about to add those items to the list when Jasper blushed some more and said, "Um ... that's not exactly what I meant."

"You are coming to Sookie's birthday party, aren't you?" The party was Saturday, and my little sister didn't exactly have a lot of friends. To be honest, all she had was me and Jasper. That was mostly my fault because I'd become all tied up in that Halloween match and she had to tag along when I was practicing almost 24/7. She never got around to making any friends at her new school. "She's counting on you."

Oh yes, and even if Sookie was only turning nine, she had a serious crush on Jasper.

"I guess ..." Jasper said drifting off in thought, as if he wasn't even sure. This was worrisome. He was always so nice to Sookie. What had changed?

"So if you aren't asking for hints for Sookie's birthday," I said, curious now, "what exactly do you mean?"

Jasper said nothing for a moment, and then as if making up his mind, he gulped. "What do girls like ... in a boy?"

The pieces of the puzzle snapped into place, and I understood why my little sister was not at all on his mind. "As in," I said, "what makes a particular girl, say, Mia, like a guy?"

Jasper gulped again.

Whoa, this wasn't going to be easy. Jasper had skipped a grade and wasn't quite thirteen like us. Being a few months younger made a huge difference in the eighth grade.

Also Jasper was a total brainiac. Guys who hung out every lunch hour in the computer lab or the library weren't the type of boys who ended up at the school dance with girls hanging off them. As far as I knew, Mia considered Jasper in the same league as my sister – sort of invisible. Certainly Mia hadn't come to understand like I had that hanging around with a smart guy had real advantages. Besides, I got the feeling Jasper wasn't looking for just another friend to hang with. Now I saw a whole other reason why he got tongue-tied whenever Mia was around.

"What do girls like about boys ... " I stalled, and then I figured out a way to let him down easy. It came to me in a flash as I thought about yesterday and all the girls that hung around Clive and Zach's table. Really it was totally obvious. "Girls like guys who are great at sports."

Jasper nodded and dropped the subject, which was a relief. Then, just as we were passing Mr. Keating's Emporium, I spotted a mysterious-looking box in the window. What a perfect birthday present for Sookie! It wasn't on the list I had just given to Jasper. Nor was it something I would have thought up – ever. But it was as if the box had Sookie's name written all over it.

"C'mon," I grabbed Jasper's arm and hauled him into the Emporium. The bell chimed as we walked through the door. Inside, the shop smelled like cinnamon, tangy apples, and fresh-baked bread, or balsawood and turpentine, depending on which side of the store you stood.

I was never quite sure how to take Mr. Keating. Sometimes I thought he was convinced I was a troublemaker. But today when he spotted me, his round face broke out into a huge smile.

"Hello, Cat. What can I do for you today?" his barrel voice boomed.

It was weird, but before I could even answer, he was reaching into the window, and I simply nodded when he brought me the box. It looked so cool – purple satin on the outside, with sparkly silver letters that spelled 101 Amazing Magic Tricks. He pulled off the lid, and I couldn't believe how many items were tucked inside. There was a book – well, more like a pamphlet – a little wand, cards, a plastic ball and cup set, some little silver triangles, some rope and dice ... I reached in to grab the instructions.

"Uh ... uh," teased Mr. Keating as he pulled back the box playfully. "Magic is very secret, so the instructions can only go to the magician."

"I don't know, Cat," Jasper whispered in my ear. "Do you really think we should be encouraging your sister – "

"How much is this?" I blurted before Jasper could finish.

"Twenty-five dollars," said Mr. Keating.

Wow, that was over my budget. Disappointed, I turned away. Then I said to Jasper as we were leaving, "I thought it would be perfect because it's strictly a kid's toy. Sookie would love it and maybe it would help, you know, make her a little happier."

Ever since my sister had her run-in with the fairies, she seemed restless. At night sometimes, I'd catch her staring up at Grim Hill, just looking out her window for hours, or other times she'd be humming eerie tunes that made the hair on the back of my neck stand up.

"You could be right," said Jasper. "If Sookie can't get Grim Hill out of her mind, maybe giving her a safe hobby of learning a few card tricks would be a good compromise."

"But it's too expensive," I sighed.

Jasper smiled. "What if we go in on it together?"

We shook hands and I went back to give Mr. Keating our combined funds. I tucked the purple box under my arm, then Jasper and I left the Emporium. We headed to the pool where I was picking Sookie up, and my happier mood made me chatty. I confided in Jasper how I thought the girls might beat the guys' team.

"We should set up a sucker trick."

"What is that?" asked Jasper.

"One of us runs to our defender as if we're going to take the ball," I said. "But instead at the last minute we give up the ball, then race in the open space and wait for the defender to kick us the pass." We knew more sophisticated strategies than the boys because of all the moves we'd learned before the Halloween match.

"Everyone at school is talking about this game, even the teachers," said Jasper. "They're calling it 'the battle of the sexes'." Jasper got that calculating look on his face. "You do know all the boys on the team will be taller and will have longer legs and more lung capacity. That means more endurance."

Somehow, the way Jasper reasoned didn't outrage me as it had with Clive and Zach. "We still have an edge on them." I tapped my head. "Strategy."

So everyone was excited about the game, and I was the one who got it going. That made me feel even better because this was an event we created ourselves. It wouldn't be fake as if everyone had fallen under some kind of spell. There was a way to be popular at Darkmont without the help of evil fairies. I started thinking of how my life at school was going to go a lot better. I got so distracted I hardly noticed when Jasper said goodbye and we parted ways at the pool. I guess we both had a lot to think about. Before he left though, I handed our gift to him. Sookie would drive me crazy all the way home demanding to see what I was carrying.

Sookie came out of the changing room a little later with her hair already dried into a golden bob. "Sunshine girl" – that's what our father always called her before he left. I was his "October girl" with dark hair and green eyes. My throat tightened as I wondered what he would think, now that I had a couple of green streaks in my hair since my fight with the fairies. We hadn't heard from our dad in awhile.

"Is it cold out?" Sookie asked. "Teacher said Father Winter is coming so we should be sure to button our coats right to the top."

"You won't need your winter gear yet," I said as Sookie dug in her pack and fussed with her mittens. "It's actually not too cold, considering it's the end of November." Except for the cloudy skies, it wasn't bad at all. As we walked back to Darkmont to meet up with Mom, Sookie babbled about learning to swim under water.

"I made it across the whole pool," she chirped.

"That's pretty far," I said doubtfully.

"Well, sideways across," she admitted. We laughed.

I dropped her off at the office with Mom. Sookie got started on her homework while she waited, and I decided to see if anything was happening on the soccer field.

The boys were practicing, so I climbed the bleachers to check out how they played – which was fast and furious, but sloppy. All power, but no control. I leaned over and watched for a while, until a soccer ball came hurtling out of nowhere and slammed me in the shoulder.

"Ow!" I shouted. Pain burned down my arm and side, making me feel dizzy and a little sick to my stomach.

22

"Cat, we're so sorry," Zach said as he came running up. "I don't know how that happened."

I quickly blinked back my tears. Then I heard a less-concerned voice beside me.

"Spies deserve what they get. And sorry, but if you're going to be playing with the big boys, you'd better toughen up."

I spun around angrily and stared at Clive's conceited face. That did it. All my guilty feelings evaporated. We were going to beat these guys, and I was going to make *him* sorry.

Then I spotted someone by the goalposts that made my stomach flip worse. "What's Jasper doing on the field?" I choked.

"He just tried out for the team," said Zach. "He's really fast. And everyone knows he's smart. We've signed him up."

"Seems some of the guys thought he could bring some strategy to our game," said Clive in a voice that hinted at my worst fears.

Good move, Cat. Tell Jasper that girls liked boys who played sports. Then let him in on a few soccer tricks. Plant your own seed of destruction. Who's the sucker now?

What exactly had I told Jasper about my soccer plans?

CHAPTER 3
Practicing Deceit

ALL NIGHT I tossed and turned in my bed as if I was sleeping on a net of soccer balls that rolled beneath me. My back and head ached as the silver light of a November morning peeked through my window shade. I kept going over yesterday in my mind and what soccer plans I'd revealed to Jasper. And then I realized I hadn't told him anything really – just one soccer trick. Nothing wrong with that. There were lots more plays besides that one – right?

Sitting down at my desk, I began to scribble down soccer strategies. The big rule was to keep the ball moving and to get it to the right person, the player who has the most time and space. That was about skill, not strength. Passing thoughtfully, dribbling with control – that would be our strategy. As I placed my pen down, I tapped it against the desk. Tap. Tap. We needed something more.

"Cat, breakfast!" Mom called.

My chair scraped against the wood floor as I teased the idea that was simmering in my head, but I had no luck. The idea stayed hidden. Maybe food would help.

Downstairs, Mom had made us waffles with sliced strawberries and bananas. I smiled at the treat, but Sookie only played with her fork.

"Can I have my cereal on top?" she asked mournfully. My little sister loved her frosty oats.

Mom sprinkled a few oats on top of Sookie's waffle to

make her happy. "So are you getting excited about your birthday party on Saturday?" Mom asked her.

"Uh ... huh ..." Sookie said with a smile.

"I was thinking, maybe we could go to a movie," Mom said.

I knew my mother was trying to plan an event that covered up the fact Sookie didn't have any friends.

"I want to play Monopoly," said Sookie. "With friends."

My heart sank. Jasper was her only friend. But now he was a traitor who had moved over to enemy territory. How would I be able to explain that to my little sister?

"We play Monopoly all the time. What if we try something different?" I suggested. "Maybe a girls' night out?"

"I'm the birthday girl, and I get to choose." Sookie got that stubborn look on her face.

That meant I'd be spending an entire Saturday afternoon entertaining my kid sister and my traitor neighbor in a boring Monopoly marathon, instead of playing soccer. Just great.

The more I thought about Jasper and the boys' team, the more I wrote and rewrote soccer strategies, so by nighttime, I actually had run out of ink in my pen. Then I spent another long night in bed as uncomfortable as the night before, trying to think of ways the girls could win. By morning I could hardly open my eyes, and it took a lot of effort to step on my icy cold bedroom floor and get ready for school.

Over night we'd had a bit of frost. As I walked Sookie to school we crunched along the frozen field, the grass icy stiff and sticking up straight like a crew cut on a giant's head.

"Jack Frost has been out painting all the grass," said Sookie. "Teacher says he paints the windows as well, announcing the arrival of winter."

I was about to mutter something about how "it's all

make-believe," but that just might be confusing to a little girl who lived in a town where pretty strange things could happen. Instead we had fun smashing the ice that glazed over the puddles, and snapping frozen grass stalks that glittered as though they'd been coated in diamonds. By the time my sister ran into the playground, the sun was beating down and the grass started wilting.

Winter wasn't here yet, plus Mom had told us it never got really cold in this area. Sookie's teacher was getting her worked up about a big winter for nothing. I began walking to Darkmont.

"Cat, wait up."

Instead, I began walking faster.

"Cat, it's me!"

Exactly. I started jogging.

"Cat?'

I left Jasper behind as I raced toward school. Then I slammed to a halt. I had this all wrong. The last thing I should do is avoid Jasper – what was that saying about keeping your enemies close? I dug my hands into the pockets of my quilted vest and waited until he reached me.

"Cat, what's up with you? I had to shout a bunch of times," Jasper's rapid breath puffed out in bursts of fog.

"I was wearing my headphones," I lied, but I patted my pocket pretending my mp3 player was inside.

Before Jasper could say anything, I started chatting. "I was thinking about soccer practice after school and how we're going to be working on our long shots." It had just occurred to me that I should feed Jasper false information. Deceiving him could be the best strategy.

"Look, Cat, you should know that I took your advice and joined the boys' soccer team." Then he grinned as if there was nothing traitorous about that, saying, "so I think we might have what you call a conflict of interest."

My advice? That he should become a spy for the boys' team? That wasn't exactly my advice. Even though he was being upfront, it irked me the way he seemed to think the whole situation was amusing. But I held my tongue and replied, "Right, um, I'll have to be more careful."

He didn't seem to notice that he was supplying all the conversation the rest of the way to Darkmont.

***

After school, the girls gathered in the gym for soccer practice; Darkmont's one scruffy field had already been taken over by the boys' team.

"How come they get the field?" complained Amarjeet. She kicked the ball hard and it slammed against the wall. The bang echoed throughout the gym.

Ms. Dreeble, who had just bustled in from class, was still slipping out of her lab coat and tying up her gym shoes. She said in a rush, "Not to worry. The office will post a gym schedule tomorrow. So let's work off our steam by playing some good soccer."

We couldn't argue with that, so for the next half hour we practiced scissor kicks and center passes. It felt good to focus strictly on physical stuff as I perfected dekeing the ball.

"Okay everyone, divide up and let's have a few soccer plays." Ms. Dreeble blew her whistle three times. "Remember, the team that moves with the ball – and that shares the ball – gets the most scoring opportunities."

Ms. Dreeble actually seemed to know something about soccer. I tried thinking about what she'd said, and as I ran, I tried to think more than one moment ahead. Instead of just kicking the ball away from my opponent, I tried spotting the player who had the best setup. This was harder than it sounded.

Girls darted in and out of my vision like flecks of color in a kaleidoscope. I knew there were patterns, but I couldn't quite spot any while I was in motion. And I couldn't stop or I'd get my feet tangled up. We thundered around the gym. Gradually, the game got contagious as the thrill of soccer worked its way through my blood again.

Quickly, I spotted Mia playing center and Emily who was her right flank. I dived for the ball and then side-angled it and watched with satisfaction as it sailed and dropped in front of Mia. Then she set Emily up for the goal. I raced ahead so fast, my lungs almost burst. But I got there just in time to run alongside Emily so that when she kicked, I could tap the ball right into the goal. This could be the beginning of a beautiful play.

"Well done!" shouted Ms. Dreeble. She spent the rest of the practice having the three of us rehearse our setup.

"Cat, a little faster – you need to keep up with Emily," she'd shout, or, "Cat you have great control of the ball, show the other girls that shot again ... and again."

"Whew, I'm winded," I said after the grueling practice.

"Me too," agreed Emily. Then, as our captain, she shouted to the rest of the team, "We should all take a few laps around the field to build up our strength!" There were no other takers, but I agreed even though I already had a stitch in my side. As Emily and I left the gym later and approached the field, we saw that the boys were still practicing. I suggested we hide underneath the bleachers.

"Last time a ball flew out of nowhere and slammed me.

I think it was a message about spying." Then I explained to Emily what had happened between me and Jasper. "So I've decided to feed him some fake strategies."

"Sweet, I love intrigue," said Emily, which made me think she still saw this whole thing only as fun. Emily pointed to one player and asked, "Who is that guy? He's pretty good."

I squinted and focused on the player who zigged and zagged swiftly around other players and appeared to set up a perfect long shot for Clive. Then I got distracted as I watched with a sinking heart as Clive made an easy kick and the ball rose high, sailed over half the field, and went straight into the net. So when the other boy – the one Emily had asked about – came closer to the bleacher, it still took a moment to recognize him. He somehow looked taller, leaner, and more muscular in a soccer shirt. Oh, and a bit older without his glasses.

"Jasper Chung?" I whispered in surprise.

"Cat," Emily said in a worried voice as she looked at her watch. "The boys have been practicing a good forty minutes longer than us. And they're still going strong."

Okay, maybe for Emily it was also about winning. And these guys had just played well.

What was it Jasper warned me about? Something about an advantage the boys had over us – something about endurance. I watched in alarm at how they weren't the least bit winded. Clearly, the girls were going to have to figure out a plan that would work against their strengths. The girls were going to have to figure out a way to make skill count the most.

CHAPTER 4

A Secret Trap

SATURDAY MORNING MOM was putting the finishing touches on the birthday cake while Sookie, who was too excited to stay still, danced around her. Mom had sliced into two layer cakes and placed them in the shape of a butterfly, which was the cake Sookie had asked for. Creamy pastel pinks with mauve swirls frosted the cake. Handing me two long pieces of red licorice ropes, I added the antennae as Sookie dotted the wings with sparkly sugar gumdrops.

"These are perfect butterfly wings," announced Sookie, who was actually quite fussy about wings in general. Butterfly wings had to have different colors, angel wings had to be white, and fairy wings had to be spotted – although technically, both Sookie and I knew that fairies didn't actually have any wings at all.

Someone tapped on the back window. Before I could fully open the door, a shiny, gold-papered present with a gigantic yellow bow was thrust into my arms.

"Jasper? Jasper Chung?" Again I was surprised. My friend had abandoned his hair spikes for a trendier faux hawk. He was wearing designer jeans. "What happened to your glasses?"

"Contacts," he said as he tapped where his glasses used to be. "For sports."

"But you're not playing soccer today – you're coming to ..." My words died on my lips as Jasper turned red.

"You are coming to Sookie's party, aren't you?" I whispered.

"There's a big practice today for the boys' team. Everyone has to show." Jasper hung his head.

"But you're her only – "

"Hi, Jasper!" Sookie had come up from behind and peeked under my arm. "You're early! We haven't got everything set up yet." Her face dimpled as she smiled.

"Um." Jasper swallowed. "I'm dropping the gift off early because I've got to be somewhere."

Sookie was going to be hurt. Jasper was letting me down – again, I thought, as blood rushed to my face.

But Sookie gave a slight shrug and said, "Okay," as if it didn't matter one little bit. She walked back and finished putting gumdrops on the cake.

Jasper let out a sigh of relief. "Catch you later," he said to me, and then he ran off before I could say anything. Personally, I thought Sookie was in shock. But when I walked back to the kitchen table, she seemed fine.

"So," I asked tentatively, "do you want to change plans and go out now?"

"Nope," said Sookie as she licked mauve frosting off a spoon.

"Sookie has a new little friend who is coming over soon," said Mom.

"That's great," I said. It was a relief that Sookie's special day wasn't going to be ruined because her one friend wasn't coming to her party. Then I realized I'd be spending the afternoon playing Monopoly with two little kids. Jasper was going to pay. But I had to at least pretend I was looking forward to the birthday celebrations, so I acted excited about not having to cancel the board game. Then I dove into preparations for the lunch in order to distract myself from thinking about Jasper.

I helped Mom make peanut butter and banana pinwheel sandwiches and deviled eggs. Just as popcorn popped in the microwave, the doorbell rang. Sookie raced off to answer it, and by the time I caught up with her, a boy about her age stood inside the living room.

"This is Skeeter," Sookie said to me. "That's my big sister, Cat," she said as she pointed up at me.

"Skeeter? That's an unusual name," I said grinning.

"Yeah, and 'Cat' isn't? At least my hair isn't striped green," the kid shot back with a glare. I felt my expression change instantly. It was going to be a long afternoon. Skeeter handed my sister a gift that had been rolled around in a pile of wrapping paper and stuck together with wads of tape. Sookie didn't seem to mind. She looked thrilled as she carried it over to the coffee table.

"Can I open my gifts now?" she called to Mom in the kitchen. Mom came out and asked for a minute, then she went into the hall closet and brought out a delicately wrapped pink parcel with frilly lace ribbons and pink rosebuds glued to the middle. That gift couldn't have looked more different from Skeeter's.

"Open mine first," begged Skeeter.

Sookie tore away the wrapping paper, revealing a plain cardboard box that had Aladdin's Lamp written on top. She ripped open the box and pulled out a blue aluminum lamp, and when she rubbed the lamp, it glowed softly. When she flicked on a tiny switch, a bulb on top got brighter.

"Ooh, thank you!" She smiled with delight.

"I picked it out myself," said Skeeter. "I also put in the batteries." He seemed so proud of himself that I warmed up to him a bit.

Then Sookie opened Mom's gift and squealed when she saw her own mp3 player, pink with little white flowers. Excitement tingled through me as I handed her the gift that Jasper – or more likely, his mother – had wrapped. "It's from Jasper and me," I emphasized.

When Sookie tore open the gift, and I must say, the elegant wrapping was lost on her – she hugged the purple satin box to her chest, and then she ran her fingers hungrily over the silver glittery letters. Opening the magic kit, she peeked inside and her face lit up as she thanked me. Even better, she and Skeeter decided they didn't want to play Monopoly after all. Instead, right after we ate, they ran upstairs to the attic to practice a few tricks so they could perform a magic show for us. Mom and I could clean up in peace. But as I wrapped up the cake in foil and put it in the fridge, we heard a huge crash in the attic.

Mom and I flew up the stairs, and when we ducked through the low door to the attic, I couldn't believe my eyes.

"What's going on here?" Mom said in her I'm-trying-not-to-sound-annoyed-but-I-really-am voice.

They'd pulled apart the whole attic. Boxes were strewn all over the floor. Every toy and game we owned had been taken off the shelves, with cards, dice, and playing pieces tossed everywhere. The magic tricks from Sookie's box were scattered all over the card table. And a big, dusty green and gold trunk – probably what had made the crash – had been pulled out.

"Skeeter thought we should look for props for the magic act," Sookie said nervously.

"Oh did he?" Mom said in that voice again. I shook my head, changing my mind back again about Skeeter. Clearly he was a bad influence.

"Sorry," Skeeter mumbled quickly, not sounding one bit sorry.

"We'll put everything back," Sookie said with a sigh.

"I'll help," I volunteered, feeling very generous because it was her birthday. And I was still grateful that at least I didn't have to play with them. We started picking up all the stuff on the floor, and while Skeeter did assist, as soon as my mother left, he got easily distracted.

"What's in here," he asked, leaning over and fiddling with the latch on the trunk.

"Don't know," I said. "It's locked."

"No it isn't." Then as bold as could be, Skeeter lifted the lid and peered inside. "Wow."

Sookie and I ran over to the trunk. It was funny – something was telling me to slam the lid down and stay away from it. When Sookie bent over and exclaimed in oohs and ahhs, I couldn't resist taking a peek. A strong scent of Christmas tree rose from the trunk. If I closed my eyes and sniffed deeply, then I would have believed I was in the middle of a forest. I helped them lift the heavy lid all the way open.

Inside, folded in tidy squares, were exotic clothes. In excitement, Skeeter heaved the lid back farther and it snapped off, falling to the floor with a smash, then a clatter.

"Sorry," said Skeeter.

"What's going on?" called Mom.

"Nothing," Skeeter, Sookie, and I shouted together.

Well, there was nothing we could do about it, so I dug in with the other two and pulled out the clothes. What had first caught our attention was a purple silk turban that had a sparkling ruby pinned in the middle, and a big black feather poking out from the brooch.

"Hey, that looks really old," said Skeeter. "Sookie, it looks like a genie hat. You should wear it when you rub the Aladdin's lamp I gave you." He reached for the turban.

"Don't touch that," I snapped. Skeeter pulled back in surprise. "I mean" – then I felt embarrassed – "be careful, it might be fragile."

Skeeter gave me a dirty look, but he shrugged and left the turban alone. Sookie, who was never slightly worried about what I said, reached in, pulled the hat out of the trunk, and set it on her head. "Very aristocratic," she observed in a dusty attic mirror.

Where did she get those words?

We fished through the rest of the trunk. There was a red bow tie and a white satin shirt. There was also a sparkly red dress, and a long, blue cape. Soon I noticed I was the only one digging through the trunk. Sookie and Skeeter were back messing with their magic tricks.

"Hey," I warned Sookie. "Careful – a magician isn't supposed to share her secrets."

"He's my assistant," was all Sookie said.

I folded up the clothes, took the turban off Sookie's head, and gently laid everything back inside the trunk. I had no idea how to put the lid back on – Skeeter had snapped the hinges – so I had to go downstairs and explain to Mom what happened.

Mom didn't appear too miffed. "I'd forgotten that trunk was up there," she said to me.

"So it's not ours?" I said trying to remember if I'd seen the movers bring it in.

"Maybe it's one of your father's items that got mixed up with our boxes," said Mom. "If Sookie and Skeeter are so curious about the trunk, it's better if the lid is off." As usual, whenever anything about Dad came up, Mom quickly changed the subject.

"Trunks can be dangerous because children can get trapped inside," said Mom. "Are you sure the lid is too heavy for those two to put it back on?"

"Trust me." I rolled my eyes. "Even Skeeter won't be able to figure out how to mess with it. It weighs a ton."

"Now, Cat," said Mom. "Boys can play more rambunctiously than girls. We're just not used to it."

Even my mother was making excuses for stupid boy behavior.

"We're ready for the show!" Sookie shouted. As she and Skeeter trudged down the stairs, magic trick kit in tow, the doorbell rang again.

When I opened the door, all I could say was –

"Not you!"

CHAPTER 5

A Slight of Hand

"**CAT, HOW IMPOLITE**," my mother said as she came up behind me. "Please come in." Mom opened the door as I stumbled backward. "Hello, I'm Mrs. Peters, and this is my daughter, Cat."

"I have the pleasure of having history class with Cat," Clive said with so much charm, I knew he was trying to upstage me. To make sure I understood, when he walked through the door and out of my mother's view, he sneered at me.

"What do you want?" My voice was flat, but polite enough. Well, perhaps not, judging by the look Mom gave me.

"I'm here to pick up my brother," Clive said.

"Skeeter is your brother?" Dismay choked off my words. Sookie, no ... not your only friend ...

"Oh good," Sookie announced from the bottom step. "We have one more person for the audience."

Skeeter nodded excitedly. He and Sookie walked to the end table, and Mom gasped as Skeeter pushed away the table near the fireplace, tipping the crystal lamp until it teetered over the edge. I leaped and grabbed the lamp just before it toppled over.

"Good reflexes," Clive chuckled.

"Hey," I said to Skeeter. "Watch it."

"Sorry," said Skeeter, a word he clearly used a lot. "We need this table for the act."

Mom and Clive were already sitting on the couch, so I chose the overstuffed chair – it was farthest away from Clive.

Sookie and Skeeter got the show under way.

"Ladies and gentlemen," Skeeter announced. "May I introduce the world's greatest magician – Sookie!"

Clive let out an annoying chuckle. Sookie stood behind the end table, and Skeeter handed her a pile of silver triangles that jingled as she tossed them on the table. She made a big show of demonstrating how the triangles were all separate.

"Now watch," Skeeter announced dramatically, "as Sookie links all the triangles together by magic."

Sookie tried containing all the triangles in her hands, but a few kept slipping through. And when she tried to pick them up again, more triangles fell between her fingers. Finally, she abandoned a couple on the end table, shook the rest in her closed fists, and when she brought her hands together and released the triangles ... they all fell back on the table, still completely separate.

Clive chuckled again.

"Glad you find us so amusing," I said.

"Cat," Mom warned.

Poor Sookie looked mortified. Skeeter seemed puzzled. "I don't know," he said to her, scratching his head. "It worked before. Maybe you should have said some of your magic words."

I squirmed uncomfortably in the chair as Sookie prepared her next trick. She was trying to rejoin a piece of rope that Skeeter had cut in half while she held the two ends taut. But the two pieces of rope dropped back on the table. I felt my face flush as I watched her provide Clive with endless amusement. Maybe the magic kit was not such a great gift.

The ball in the cup dropped to the floor and rolled under the couch, which was the only way Sookie could make it disappear. When she poured water into a vase, it leaked all over the carpet. Finally, Mom put an end to the agony when she got up and said, "Why don't I get Clive and Skeeter some cake to take home."

I sighed in relief, but as soon as Mom left, Sookie threw her magic box down in total disgust. Skeeter started scooping all the spilled tricks back into the box. "Don't give up," he told her. "You can do it."

"But that's where you two have got it all wrong," said Clive, standing up from the couch.

"What do you mean?" asked Sookie.

"You've got it backwards. David Copperfield, Blackstone, Houdini – guys are supposed to be the magicians. Girls are supposed to be the ones who get sawed in half."

Sookie looked crushed, and I got ready to tell Clive off. But Skeeter came to the rescue.

"You're wrong, Clive. Sookie is a really good magician."

Clive shrugged his shoulders. "I'm just saying that if you switched places, the act would probably work better. Name some famous women magicians." Clive looked so sure of himself when I couldn't name even one. Just then, Mom came back with a plate of birthday cake wrapped up for Clive and Skeeter. As I walked with them to the porch, grateful that the two boys were finally leaving, I overheard Skeeter talking to his brother.

"I don't care what you say, Clive. Sookie is the best magician. I like being the assistant."

Sookie's new friend was all right – for a boy.

As soon as I stepped back inside, I said, "Okay, Sookie, let's go on the computer and look up famous women magicians." But Sookie didn't seem that interested. Instead she was looking sadly at her box of magic tricks. "I don't understand," she was saying as she flipped through the pamphlet. "It worked before. What did I do wrong?"

"You can't always be good at something right away. It takes practice." But even as I said that a faint shiver went up my back, as if it wasn't really good advice I was giving her. I shook it off and went to turn on the computer in the den. After typing in "famous women magicians," the name Adelaide Herrmann, Queen of Magic, came up. "Hey, Sookie, take a look at this. I wonder what a conjurer is." Then, I pulled up the Queen of Magic's bio.

The phone rang. It was Mia telling me that the boys had finally abandoned the soccer field and we could use it now for practice. I rushed out the front door, leaving the picture of Adelaide Herrmann on the screen. It was a spooky poster of a woman standing beside a Greek column. She held a sword, and a decapitated head sat on top of the column. Skeletons floated all around.

But only soccer was on my mind.

When I arrived on the soccer field, I looked at the uniforms Mia and Amarjeet were handing out. They were nowhere near as dazzling as the soccer outfits we wore for the Halloween match. Funny, every day that event seemed to shrink in my mind as if it had happened a couple of years back instead of only a month ago. As for our Darkmont uniforms, we provided our own white shorts and were given the boys' old jerseys that were yellow and red – but the red stripe had faded to orange. We did get new red and yellow socks that matched the jerseys – sort of.

Trying to warm up my muscles, I joined the other girls and began running around the field.

"Faster everyone!" shouted Ms. Dreeble, who abandoned the sidelines and began running with us. "After four laps, we'll take some shots on goal."

During the Halloween match, soccer played me as if I was a violin and the rhythm of the game plucked itself on my strings. All my senses came alive, and I could feel things more than any ordinary person. I admit that maybe it was a little like being a puppet dangled on a string. But for the moment, it seemed better than what I was experiencing now – shin splints. The only thing I saw now was heavy gray skies. And the only thing I smelled – come to think of it, I didn't smell a thing because my nose was plugged up. But hard work paid off, and while my kicks weren't exactly magical, I did manage to get a few balls past the goalie. Another thing that was very different preparing for this match was that my energy wasn't boundless. After an hour and a half of soccer practice, Mia, Amarjeet, and I dragged ourselves home. Muddy and sore, I couldn't wait for a hot bath.

"We've got the soccer field for two practices during the week, and for next Saturday afternoon!" Ms. Dreeble called after us.

The match was creeping up fast. Only three more practices and the game would be the following Monday. Time to step up feeding Jasper more misinformation. As I discussed with Mia and Amarjeet how we could sabotage the boys' soccer practice, Emily joined us.

"We really should keep up with our running," she said.

I glanced at Emily's long legs and thought, easy for you to say, but I said, "Maybe tomorrow?" Mia and Amarjeet seemed even less enthusiastic, muttering something about "other plans."

When I got home, Mom had dinner ready: tacos – birthday girl's choice. Sookie had regained her happy mood and dug into her taco after she loaded it up with a lion's share of shredded cheese and hardly any lettuce or tomatoes.

"So, you had a good birthday?" Mom smiled hopefully. I could tell this was important to her because our lives were so different from before our parents' divorce. There was no money in the budget for laser tag or one of those parties where you went to a store to build your own fancy teddy bear – activities like that might have actually lured a few friends into coming to Sookie's party.

"Best birthday ever." Sookie nodded enthusiastically and then crunched into her gigantic taco. Most of the filling fell out of the other end and scattered on the table.

I was glad she was no longer frustrated by the gift I'd given her. When Mom asked her if she wanted to watch a DVD after dinner – some cartoon princess movie – she said, "No. I'm going back up to the attic to practice my magic."

"Uh, Sookie," I advised, "are you sure you want to get into that again? Besides, your assistant has gone home. I mean, look at me – I'm beat after all my soccer today, and I'm sure if I tried practicing, I'd just get frustrated." Mom nodded in agreement.

"First of all," Sookie said firmly, "I'm no longer just 'Sookie.' I'm 'Sookie, Queen of Mystery.' And I figured out what I was doing wrong this afternoon," she said, looking a bit mysterious.

"Your choice – you're the birthday girl," Mom agreed. "But it's getting late. How about having your bath first, and then you can practice with your magic kit in your room."

"Can I bring down some of the clothes from the trunk?" asked Sookie.

Mom nodded.

Sookie shot her hand up in the air and said, "Yes!"

I sure hoped by tomorrow when her birthday was over that she wasn't going to expect having everything her way.

Later, as Sookie practiced magic in her room after washing up, I could finally get around to jumping into a hot bath myself. I dumped in a ton of bubble foam – jasmine, my favorite. After I settled in the tub, I turned on more hot water until steam coated the bathroom mirror and tiles. The fragrant water seeped deep into my sore muscles. With my finger, I carved xs and os into the suds, imagining soccer plays. After my bath, I wrapped myself in Mom's thick chenille bathrobe. Pattering down the hall to my bedroom, I could hear talking from my sister's room.

I tapped lightly on the door, but when Sookie didn't answer, I cracked it open and checked inside. The purple turban with the black feather and sparkling ruby sat lopsided on the Queen of Mystery's head. She was holding cards in her hand and she was mumbling odd words.

"Ahem," I said, trying to get her attention.

Sookie's head jerked toward me. "Get out!" she shouted.

I quickly backed away from her room. Then, more like her usual self, Sookie jumped up, the turban slipping off her head and tumbling to the floor. "Sorry. It's just that magicians need to keep their secrets, and I was trying to conjure."

Not about to admit to my kid sister that I didn't exactly know what conjuring was, I simply nodded and closed the door. But as I began to walk away, a ray of pale green light oozed out from under Sookie's door. I knocked again and stepped inside.

"What's making that weird-colored light?" I asked. Weird wasn't exactly the right word ... more like eerie.

"My new Aladdin's lamp," Sookie said quickly.

"Oh, right." I slipped out again, shutting her door. Once in the privacy of my room, I recalled looking in the box and I didn't remember seeing different-colored bulbs for the lamp. Shrugging my shoulders, I grabbed my dictionary off my desk and looked up the word "conjure": To summon by magical incantation.

What exactly was Sookie trying to summon?

Just then I heard a strange loud pop and a buzz.

My bedroom light flashed and then went out.

CHAPTER 6

The Demon Handkerchief

THE WHOLE HOUSE plunged into darkness. My heart thumped as I scrambled to find a candle in my room. But what good was a candle when I didn't have any matches? Although the day had been reasonably mild, the wind now howled in shrill blasts, and a bitter draft made its way through the window pane. Blood pumped loudly in my ears, so I missed the pitter patter of steps down the hall. I jumped back and my heart thumped when a ghostly face hovered in my doorway.

Gasping, I realized it was only Sookie. Her face was illuminated by the spooky pale light of her Aladdin's lamp.

"Power's gone out," she said coolly.

Pulling myself together, and determined to be braver than my kid sister, I forced a calm expression. Sookie was never scared of the dark. Of course, I wasn't either; I just didn't like it much. Swallowing my nerves, I went downstairs with Sookie. Her lamp lit our way.

A thread of light bobbed, and Mom came out of the kitchen carrying a flashlight. "It's not just our house – it looks like the power is out on our entire block." She went into the hall closet and put on her wool coat and thickest scarf. "I'm just going to check out the next street."

Shivering, Sookie and I went with her onto the porch as the frigid air slapped our skin. Ice covered everything and the telephone lines sagged. Some branches had snapped off the trees. A power line had broken from a transformer and the wire dangled in the front of our house, writhing like an enraged cobra spitting blue and yellow sparks into the night.

"Oh my gosh, get back in the house!" Mom warned. "A downed line can be deadly. I'll go out back and listen to the news on the car radio."

Sookie and I huddled on the couch and waited. What a time for the furnace to cut out. We pulled the scratchy wool afghan over us and kept our feet off the cold floor. Mom eventually returned carrying a pile of firewood and the barbecue lighter. I helped her start a fire in the fireplace while she explained what she'd heard on the radio.

"This is bizarre," she said. "An ice storm has hit. The ice has brought down most of the main power lines."

I lit some newspaper, placed it in the fireplace on the grate, and blew the tiny red embers until the kindling burst into flame. Inhaling the wood smoke, I asked. "Why is that bizarre?"

"This town rarely gets any cold weather," said Mom. "And yet, we got the storm even though it missed the city, which is farther north."

Yellow flames danced in the hearth. "It's fortunate, though, that we're the only area that's been hit," Mom continued. "The power company is able to send workers right away to fix our lines. We should have the electricity restored late tomorrow night."

That didn't sound so fortunate to me because that meant school would be on as usual come Monday. Mom allowed us to drag our quilts down to the living room, and we camped out by the fire. But even that drove me nuts as Sookie wouldn't stop reading by her Aladdin's lamp. It kept shining in my face all night. When Mom finally made her turn the lamp off, Sookie pestered me, whispering over and over how her magic tricks now worked.

"That's great," I muttered in exhaustion, my eyelids drooping as if they were tied to sacks of cement. "Glad it's working out." Then I drifted to sleep as her voice chattered away, fading into my dreams. She was going on and on about how magic was really all about secrets ... or something like that.

***

True to the power company's word, the electricity was quickly restored on Sunday. When Monday morning came, the classrooms were buzzing as everyone talked about the storm; it seemed as if our town never had what one teacher called "severely inclement weather" in the fall.

"We froze," complained Mia. "My little sister and I had to wear our coats and hats to bed!"

"We had to have cold soup for dinner," agreed Amarjeet.

I guessed the ice storm was a lot harder on people who didn't have fireplaces. By noon on Monday, the sun came out again and warmed the outdoors, but the rays had turned the frozen soccer field to mush. So, despite the soccer schedule our principal, Ms. Severn, had posted on the gym door, both the girls' and boys' teams had to crowd into the gym after school for indoor soccer.

Confined to one half of the gymnasium, I whispered to the other girls, "Look, we're not going to get a decent workout anyway, so why not put on a little show?"

"What do you mean?" asked Emily as her forehead wrinkled and the corners of her mouth tugged down into what was maybe going to be a frown.

"I say we play badly," I continued, despite her disapproving look. "We miss balls, shoot wildly, and basically trick the boys into thinking we won't be any challenge to them at all."

Mia and Amarjeet giggled and then agreed with enthusiasm.

"I don't know ..." Emily scanned the gym. "We need to build up our leg muscles – soccer's all about running without getting winded."

"All we'll get is dizzy running around half a gym." Amanda joined our huddle. "So we might as well make better use of our time."

"Well?" I asked with an evil grin.

Emily managed to look a bit wicked herself. "I guess it could be fun."

Like a shot we were off, scrambling around in crazy formations, missing balls, tripping over our feet. The boys' practice slowed as they turned to watch. Enjoying their attention, we goofed off even more. When they laughed and began to imitate us, we knew we weren't fooling anybody. But it was all too much fun to resist. Soon both the boys and girls were playing together, stumbling around, and bouncing volley balls, tennis balls, and any kind of ball we could find onto the gleaming wood floor. Zach and Jasper began shooting a soccer ball through a basketball hoop. Our entire practice disintegrated into madness, and soon I found myself inside a circle of flying dodge balls. Even though no one was throwing hard, the soccer balls hurt pretty bad if they hit you.

A shrill whistle blasted our ears. We all stopped and turned as Mr. Morrows and Ms. Dreeble scowled at us. Our laugher died away, and there was only the sound of us shuffling around.

"This is what I'm giving up my time for?" Ms. Dreeble shook her head in disbelief, removing her thick glasses before they slid down her nose.

"Do you really think you can spare precious practice time?" Mr. Morrows glared at the boys, his mustache twitching. "I thought you cared about winning the intramurals." Jasper looked horrified. Clearly he wasn't used to upsetting teachers.

After a lecture about discipline and how people who succeeded had to maintain their focus, we were all dismissed. Seems that the teachers didn't think the gym should be kept open late for what Mr. Morrows called "chicanery resulting in injury." As we piled out of the school and began heading home, I heard a disgruntled voice from behind.

"Whose bright idea was that anyway?"

Clive had stepped out of the crowd and was staring suspiciously at me. It didn't help that Mia and Emily's eyes shifted in my direction.

"I thought so," complained Clive. "You are nothing but trouble with your punk hairstyle and bad attitude."

Where did that come from? I spun around, ready to lay into him about how everyone seemed more than happy to join in and fool around in the gym, but come to think of it, I hadn't actually seen Clive participate. So all I managed was to say, "For your information, those green streaks in my hair are my natural color."

"That's what I'd expect someone like you to say," Clive said dismissively.

What was his problem? "Maybe you're getting a little worried about the match."

But Clive snapped, "Who cares about the match? What I don't want is to lose the intramurals."

"Well who said you're the one who is going to the intra-murals in the first place?" I shouted back. And so what – I'd gotten a little sidetracked. But all of a sudden I squirmed uncomfortably. Clive had a way of getting to me. Not wanting to give him an ounce of satisfaction, I waited until he stormed off, leaving everyone behind. Then I talked Mia and Emily into coming with me to apologize to Ms. Dreeble. It was a smart move because our teacher seemed satisfied as we promised to work a lot harder. Also, I think it helped that Emily volunteered us to gather up all the balls on the gym floor and put the soccer nets away.

It was getting dark by the time I got home, and I was looking forward to whatever Mom would be making for dinner. But when I opened the door, I was completely disori-ented as I stared into our crowded living room. About a dozen little kids were sitting all over the furniture, tables, and floor. More disconcerting, Clive and Jasper were sitting on each end of the couch, and Mom sat between them. When did we become a rec center for all these little kids? And I could really live without Clive and Jasper hanging out here too.

Skeeter and the Queen of Mystery were about to dazzle the crowd with a magic show. They had somehow managed to drag the trunk down from the attic and they'd turned it upside down to set it up as a prop – a table for their magic tricks. Sookie had used glitter pens and dotted the blue cape with sparkly stars and moons. She'd draped the cape over the top of the trunk like a table cloth. I found a spot on the wool rug as Sookie prepared to perform.

In a way, I didn't want to watch the show, and I wished I could just go to my room and do homework. But I knew that would hurt my sister. What if Sookie's act turned into another disaster – and in front of all these kids? They wouldn't be as understanding as her little friend Skeeter. Worse yet, I didn't want her to provide any more amusement for Clive. The part I didn't get was whether this was about my pride or Sookie's.

My sister looked kind of silly in that huge purple turban that slipped back and forth on her head. And she almost tripped on the glittery red dress she wore. Skeeter wore the stiff white shirt and red bow tie. He stood proudly in front of the end table. Clearly they thought they looked professional.

"The Queen of Mystery will now perform the Demon Handkerchief trick," Skeeter announced with a large sweep of his arm, before jumping out of my sister's way.

Sookie shook out a large green handkerchief. Skeeter announced in an ominous tone, "Whatever is placed in the demon handkerchief will never be seen again." Then Skeeter produced a plastic gold coin from his pocket and handed it to Sookie.

The Queen of Mystery folded the handkerchief over the coin, put the handkerchief on the trunk, and then she spoke to the handkerchief saying, "Bow-la." I thought to myself, Woops, she means "voila," as I'd heard other magicians say. She lifted the handkerchief up right away. The coin was gone. Not bad, I thought. Jasper got on his hands and knees and checked under the table and behind Sookie and Skeeter, but I hadn't heard anything drop. A few of the kids clapped. Next, Skeeter flashed a large card in front of the audience – the Queen of Diamonds. Again, Sookie slipped the handkerchief over the card, said, "Bow-la," and again placed it on top of the trunk. She instantly shook the handkerchief, opened it ... and the card couldn't be found! Now everyone clapped.

Next, Skeeter came out of the kitchen holding an egg. Mom frowned slightly, but she didn't interrupt their act. After tucking the egg into the silk handkerchief, Sookie placed the wrapped egg on the trunk. When she shook the handkerchief again and said her magic words, she let go of one end. The kids closest to her expected an egg to come hurtling forward, so they tried to dodge. I gulped.

The egg had disappeared!

This time I clapped along with everyone else. Just as Skeeter was about to hand Sookie one of my mother's fancy china teacups, the doorbell rang. Mom stood up. "That was wonderful, but it sounds like parents are arriving to take everyone home." I noticed she took back her teacup quickly.

As the kids filed out, I heard Clive say to Skeeter, "Not bad, but you do know a magician is supposed to bring back the object that's disappeared, right?"

"We can't yet," said Skeeter. "But Sookie thinks she'll figure it out."

Clive scowled as he herded his brother to the door. "You could learn the trick."

"Not like Sookie."

The way Skeeter said that sent chills up and down my arms for some reason. But then I couldn't resist bugging Clive. "What's the matter with you? Seems your little brother thinks girls can make good magicians."

"Well, Sookie is a good magician," Skeeter said, and then he added in a curious tone, "So what? What does Cat mean?" he asked Clive.

Clive put his arm around Skeeter's shoulder and again rattled off the names of Harry Houdini and Blackstone. But as they walked off, I could hear Skeeter insisting he still liked being the assistant. What an ego Clive had, pressuring his brother like that.

Jasper lingered behind after the kids had gone. "I'm glad you liked our birthday present," he said to Sookie.

Her face dimpled and she nodded. "Yeah – it's really fun."

"Actually, I think we've created a monster," I joked to Jasper. But then I remembered he was a traitor, and I wished he'd leave.

Jasper went over to the trunk and asked if he could look at the demon handkerchief. Sookie handed it to him.

"Hey," I said. "I thought magicians weren't supposed to give away their secrets."

"I'm not." Sookie looked a bit sly.

"I don't get it," Jasper said quietly. He held up the handkerchief. "I know this trick. There's supposed to be two handkerchiefs sewn together, one with a slit in it. But this is only one handkerchief and there's no hole to slip the objects through. I can't figure out how you made those things disappear?"

Sookie beamed proudly.

Jasper shook his head. "Besides, your hands are tiny and your costume doesn't even have sleeves to hide an egg or a coin." Jasper took the blue cape off the top of the trunk.

Weird, Sookie and Skeeter had not turned the trunk upside down as I'd thought. The open trunk sat there, and I wondered how they'd managed to balance the blue cape on top without it caving in. Also, I couldn't see the coin, card, or egg inside the trunk.

Jasper shook his head and turned to me. "What is your sister up to?"

CHAPTER 7

Magic is Secret

SOOKIE LOOKED DISTRESSED. "What do you mean, Jasper? This is just magic. I'm practicing to become a conjurer like the famous Queen of Magic, Adelaide Herrmann."

Her eyes began to tear up and threatened to spill down her cheeks. I couldn't just stand there and watch Jasper hurt Sookie's feelings.

"What are you talking about?" I said to him. "It's some kind of sucker trick. Sookie and Skeeter are obviously sneaking the objects into the trunk when the audience isn't watching." Still, I wondered how those two kept the cloth on top of the trunk from caving in. Reaching over, I grabbed the midnight-blue cape. "This material is stiff; they pull the cape tight, so it sits on the top of the trunk – then they sneak the objects underneath it and into the trunk."

I could tell Jasper was trying hard to figure this out, because he reached to shove his glasses up on his forehead like he always did when he concentrated, but there were no glasses anymore. Instead he scratched his head. "Once the things landed in the trunk, where did they go?"

Sookie turned red. "It's a magician's secret." I could tell by the set of her mouth that Jasper wouldn't find anything out.

"Listen," I reasoned, "isn't that the point of a sucker trick – to make you think you know what's happening, and

53

then you realize you don't?" Kind of like trusting your friend and never expecting him to take sides with the enemy, I thought to myself.

"We weren't expecting them to perform their tricks over an open trunk – so I'm sure we just didn't see them drop the objects inside the trunk under the cape. Then Skeeter probably ditched the stuff." I imagined somewhere there'd be a smashed egg, a torn card, and a coin dropped down a heat register. Good thing Mom had grabbed her tea cup back.

"I guess ..." Jasper admitted. "Well, you're an excellent magician." Jasper patted Sookie on the shoulder. This time she turned pink from his praise. "Magic is cool. And hey, I never heard of Adelaide Herrmann."

"Of course not, because she was a woman," I said in as offended of a voice as I could muster. "It's easy for guys to say they're better if no one ever acknowledges what girls accomplish." This came out with a lot of passion, which I wasn't sure was fair – considering I'd never heard of the Queen of Magic before I'd Googled "women magicians." So what? That didn't make me wrong. I glared at Jasper.

"Look, Cat, I had nothing to do with the boys teasing all of you about your soccer skills." Jasper sounded earnest. "Remember, I've watched all of you play. We're going to have a tough time competing against your team."

"Well, you've made it tougher by running to the boys' team and spilling our secrets!" I shouted. There, I said it.

"But I didn't." Jasper's mouth dropped in surprise. "Why would you even think that?"

"Because you're a traitor," I shouted. For some reason I wanted Jasper to only be on my side all the time – not Zach's, not Clive's, and not even Mia's.

"I'd better go," was all Jasper said, and then he left. As

he slammed the door, an icy gust of air blasted. I don't think the frigid wind was the only thing that left me shivering.

"Are you mad at Jasper?" Sookie asked.

"Yeah, a bit," I confessed.

"Hope you work it out," she said, and then she turned away. It was funny – she didn't seem that upset. A month ago, she'd have driven me crazy, pestering me to make up with our friend.

"Strange," Mom observed as she came back into the living room. "The weather warmed up considerably this afternoon, and now the temperature has plunged again. Well, we'd better tidy up," she said to Sookie. I watched with surprise as she and Sookie easily pushed the trunk out of the living room and into the den. Then as if the trunk was as light as a feather, they stood it up on its side in the corner.

"How did you do that?" I asked. Hurrying over, I easily tipped the trunk away from the wall and pushed it back.

"It must be made out of a very light plastic," Mom said. "Only the lid of the trunk was heavy."

"Heavy as a giant rock," agreed Sookie.

"But I insisted we remove the lid for safety," Mom said.

"Because trunks with lids are dangerous," repeated Sookie.

Why did it seem to me that the trunk still wasn't exactly safe? I decided that didn't make sense, especially if Mom thought it was okay for Sookie to play with it.

The phone rang and it was for Sookie. She took the call in the kitchen so Mom and I couldn't hear her and Skeeter planning their next magic show. That's why she didn't care as much about my fight with Jasper. My little sister finally found her own social life. Was I disappointed that suddenly I was pushed away like some old doll or teddy bear gathering dust on her shelf?

Not at all.

The next day at school, whenever I saw Jasper near my locker or in the cafeteria, we looked away from each other and we didn't speak – there wasn't even a muttered hello. The sun came out again in the morning, and by three o'clock, the soccer field was nothing but porridge. But this time, there was a new soccer schedule posted on the wall, and the girls got the whole gym. Until the weather improved we were going to get to use the gym on alternate days, and the boys were going to have to wait until tomorrow to practice. As the guys stood around in the hall complaining, the girls piled into the gym and started kicking the balls around.

"We better make good use of our time!" shouted Emily. Our team captain ordered us to run laps, and when Ms. Dreeble came in, she nodded in approval.

We thundered like a herd of horses trampling across the gym floor.

"It's no good," complained Emily. "The gym's too small. We're not getting enough distance to build up our endurance."

Endurance – why did I lock onto that word? It suddenly seemed urgent to find out more about how the boys' team was really doing.

CHAPTER 8

The Magic Cauldron

THE NEXT DAY after school I cornered Mia at her locker and suggested, "Why don't we sneak backstage in the gym and watch the boys practice soccer?"

"Spy on the guys? I'm in." She tossed her books into her locker. We tried talking Amarjeet and Emily into joining us.

"Can't," said Amarjeet. "My brother's helping with some big magic show after school." She frowned. "My mother's busy, so she says I have to bring him."

"Oh, right," Mia made a face. "My little sister has been going on and on about it, and she keeps bugging me to download spooky music on my mp3 for the show. She also took our flashlight, which isn't cool – with this weather, who knows when the lights will go out again."

"I've heard about those shows," said Emily as she tucked a strand of golden hair behind her ear. "Even the kids I babysit talk about them."

I wondered if I should say that it was my sister who was the star, but I decided to hold off, mostly because I wasn't sure I was so crazy about my sister becoming a "Queen of Mystery." Still, it seemed my sister was turning into one of the most popular kids of the younger set. I felt a warm rush of happiness that this was all because of me. I'd found the magic kit for her, even if she'd already gone beyond the little kid tricks in that purple satin box and – in her own Sookie way – was going over the top.

"C'mon, Cat." Mia shook me out of my thoughts. We sneaked into the gym before the boys arrived for their indoor practice.

As long as the weird fluctuating weather held out, practices would be held in the gym. In the morning we were in the depths of a winter chill, but by noon the sun shone fiercely, warming the ground until the ice melted. The field kept turning to mush. Then late in the afternoon, the temperature plunged into another deep freeze. There was nothing on record for this kind of weather, and the peculiar arctic stream was only flowing into our town.

The boys streamed in from outside, so we hid behind a green velvet curtain. It was pretty dusty, so I held my nose and tried not to sneeze when the boys began to kick balls around. Then I tried not to laugh because all they did was try to hit each other with the balls and knock each other off the benches. For half an hour they clowned around. All except for Clive. I couldn't help but notice that he spent the entire time focused on kicking a ball across the gym and into the net. When Mr. Morrows arrived, the boys got down to serious soccer. But it was almost as if the gym couldn't contain their energy. Their balls shot way over their marks and often bounced wildly off the gym walls. The boys slammed into each other as they ran full force toward the goal net. This could be a bonus for the girls.

"You know," I said to Mia, finally remembering Jasper had warned me about how the boys could win with their endurance, "this weather could really work in our favor. Monday's big match has been scheduled to take place inside the gym. And that means the boys strength could work against them. We won't have to worry about their stamina." The boys were doomed. When Mia didn't respond, I looked over my shoulder at her.

Suddenly I didn't think Mia had come to spy on the boys' soccer plays at all. With a silly smile pasted on her face, she'd become super-focused on one player. Every play Mitch made, Mia watched in awe. I got a peculiar lump in my stomach. Poor Jasper. She hadn't glanced over at him once, even with his cool new haircut and contact lenses. Although we were fighting, I couldn't help but think how disappointed he'd feel.

By the time the boys' practice finished, my neck ached from staying in one position for over an hour, and my nose was seriously stuffed up. Stretching out our cramped muscles, Mia and I took the back exit from the gym and managed to escape undetected. The sun had almost set by the time we left the school. We walked home as the sun sank in a frigid lavender sky. It was only a few more weeks until winter break, and we thought we might actually have a white Christmas. That would be cool. I wound my wool scarf tighter around my neck and dug my hands into my pockets. A bitter wind shrilled past, nibbling me with its icy blasts.

"I've never felt so cold," Mia said between chattering teeth. We were about to part at my street when we noticed a steady stream of kids walking up the stairs to my house. Mia turned to me, looking puzzled.

"You may as well know," I finally confessed. "The magic shows are run by my little sister, also known as The Queen of Mystery."

Mia's eyebrows shot up. "Well, she always was a little – "

"A little what?" I quickly said.

"Um ... not peculiar. I wasn't about to say peculiar," she chuckled.

Mia's laugh didn't sound mean, so I joined her. Besides,

Sookie would be the first one to agree she was unique. My little sister was one of those kids who couldn't care less what everyone thought about her. This sudden fame was actually quite wasted on her, I thought wistfully.

I invited Mia to the show, and we stepped inside the warmth of my house, dumping our scarves and coats on top of the gigantic pile of jackets and boots next to the door. The living room was standing room only. Sookie's show was crammed to capacity. Then I spotted Amarjeet, who had to bring her little brother. When she saw me, she rolled her eyes and shook her head, basically to let me know that she had better things to do than watch my kid sister's magic show. Sookie's popularity was out of my hands, so I could only come up with a sympathetic grin.

The doorbell rang and I opened the door to Jasper and Clive. I couldn't resist saying, "You guys just can't miss a third-grader's party, can you?"

Clive shot me a look of pure dislike and said, "I'm here to pick up my brother again." Jasper didn't bother offering any explanation.

The kids began the act, and our living room light dimmed as the flashlight-turned-spotlight shone on Sookie, Queen of Mystery. I hung out near the coffee table, and even though the room was dark, I noticed Jasper give side-glances to Mia. Unfortunately, Mia didn't even look his way as she forced her little sister, Toni, to make some room for her in our wingback chair.

This time, Sookie took off her silly purple turban and set it on the blue cloth draped over the smoky-green trunk.

"This trick is called the Demon's Cauldron," Skeeter announced. "Except," he giggled, "we're gonna use Sookie's turban as a cauldron."

The upbeat kiddy song about wheels going "round and round" played in the background. That made more sense when Skeeter produced a small wire cage, and inside, Sookie's hamster spun around on his little wheel. Buddy then leaped off his wheel, poked his tiny pink nose through the bars, and sniffed wildly with curiosity. What were Sookie and Skeeter up to? I wouldn't appreciate scrambling under chairs, kids, and couches searching for a hamster on the loose.

Sookie lifted open the door to Buddy's cage and gently grasped her hamster. She set him inside the turban. She then set the turban on the trunk and everyone went, "Ah ... so cute ..." as Buddy put his tiny paws on the rim on the turban and peeked out at everyone. Then Sookie said "Bow-la," spun the turban like a top, and turned it upside down.

No hamster dropped out.

Buddy had disappeared.

Everyone gasped, and Toni shouted, "Where did he go?"

I replayed the trick in my mind, but Sookie had been incredibly fast. The blue scarf hadn't moved – I was sure of it – and Sookie's sparkly red dress didn't have long sleeves to hide a little fuzz ball. It must have been Skeeter, I decided. But I couldn't remember if he'd even been near the turban. As I puzzled over the details, Skeeter said excitedly, "And now for the best part of the trick."

Sookie furrowed her brow in concentration, and I didn't like it one bit when she began to hum that eerie song I heard coming from her room sometimes. That tune made my skin prickle. She said a strange word. It sounded something like foo- thee – and yet both that word and the tune sounded vaguely familiar. She tipped the turban upside down. Suddenly, Buddy stuck his nose out of the turban, then the rest of his body slowly scrambled up over the edge and everyone clapped.

"How did you do that?" Clive was already at the trunk and grilling his brother.

"Why do you assume Skeeter had anything to do with it," I asked, even though I myself was also wondering what his role had been.

"Magicians never reveal their secrets," Sookie and Skeeter chimed together.

A little later, as everyone got ready to leave, Mia and Amarjeet told me the show was pretty good. But I could tell Amarjeet would rather be doing her own thing than dragging her brother around. After the other kids left, Jasper lingered near the front door.

"There's something not right about these magic shows, Cat."

CHAPTER 9

The Secret Switch

"**MAGIC TRICKS USED** to be my hobby," Jasper explained. "There are only a few ways to make something disappear – trap doors, mirrors, or hiding the object in a cape or up a long sleeve. Sookie didn't use any of those things."

"Well there must be some other way Sookie made her hamster disappear and reappear since we just saw it happen," I argued.

Jasper shook his head. "I've read about two kinds of magic. There's the art of illusion and then there's something called black magic."

I understood that creating an illusion meant tricking the audience into thinking something happened when it didn't, but I never heard of black magic. "What is black magic?"

"Magic by unnatural means," said Jasper.

I could feel the alarm rising inside me because I had been witness to unnatural things, and I didn't care for that experience much. "Could you be a little clearer?"

"Black magic is when a person can use the supernatural to influence people, objects, or animals ... hamsters, for example."

"You mean Sookie used the supernatural to make Buddy and the other objects disappear? I doubt it – how could she do that?"

"Because there is another explanation for black magic," whispered Jasper.

The hair on my arms started prickling when I asked, "What's the explanation?"

"Black magic has been linked to fairies."

I didn't want to even think about that, but just in case, I said, "Maybe it's time we paid a visit to Alice and Lucinda Greystone."

"Is now okay?" Jasper wasn't wasting any time.

"Mom," I called out. "Jasper and I will be back soon."

"Dinner is in an hour," she yelled from the kitchen.

Outside the temperature had taken a serious plunge, and our breath came out in icy puffs as we rushed to the Greystone sisters' house. Alice Greystone had spent all her years longing for a sister she could never remember. Poor Lucinda missed out on a whole life. But because of their encounters with wicked fairies, they were likely to know if there was trouble brewing again on Grim Hill.

We turned down their street, spotted their old-fashioned house, climbed the stairs, and banged the brass lion's head door knocker.

"Look at all the junk mail on the porch," said Jasper. "I don't think anyone's home."

Standing outside and shivering in the cold, it suddenly seemed stupid to be running around looking for explanations about black magic.

"Jasper, I'm going home," I complained. "It seems to me that if you start looking for something, you'll see it everywhere. If we start thinking fairies are at the bottom of every weird event, next thing you know we'll think they're the cause of everything. Soon we'll be saying they are responsible for this strange weather."

"Exactly!" shouted Jasper as I began walking home.

When I got to my house, I walked into the middle of

a catastrophe.

"Buddy's sick! Something's wrong with Buddy!" Sookie shrieked as tears spilled from her eyes. She was holding her hamster ever so gently in her hands. Buddy lay still, eyes closed, and not even his little nose twitched.

"Maybe he's dizzy and is feeling a little sick from the magic trick – you did spin him around in that turban," I suggested, rather helpfully, in my mind.

"I doubt it." Sookie's voice was thick with worry. "Buddy spins himself silly in his wheel all day. He likes it. Maybe he's getting a cold. We have to take him to the vet," Sookie said as Mom hovered over her shoulder.

Mom got a look on her face – like when she has to dispose of a poor dead bird or mouse we occasionally find in the backyard. That look meant she didn't like what she had to do one bit, but nevertheless she braced herself.

She crouched next to Sookie and said, "Sweetheart, vets are very expensive – sometimes hundreds of dollars. And a little hamster is – "

"A member of our family," wailed Sookie.

I edged up next to my sister and tentatively brushed the tip of my finger over Buddy. "His fur feels silky, and soft, not stiff ... and he's warm." I knew from my own hamster experiences that those were good signs.

Sookie looked up at Mom with glistening eyes. "Please do something."

"First," said Mom in an adult's reassuring voice that probably fooled Sookie, "let's make Buddy very comfortable. Get his cage, and I'll put some nice soft shredded tissue in the bottom for a comfy bed."

Sookie scurried off. Moments later she came back with Buddy's cage and helped me and Mom shred a fresh nest for the hamster. Then we tucked Buddy in, and Sookie hugged the cage as she placed it next to the kitchen radiator where he'd be nice and warm. Mom placed a tea towel over the cage.

"We could call Amarjeet's mom," I suggested. "I think she's a vet assistant."

Mom got on the phone while Sookie and I sat down to dinner. Let's just say no one seemed very hungry, even though it was veggie burgers and oven fries. We were waiting for Mrs. Singh to drop by. When she arrived, she examined Buddy under Sookie's watchful eye.

"Well, he really does just seem to be sleeping," she pronounced. "But it is a concern that I can't rouse him."

Sookie paled.

"However," said Mrs. Singh, patting Sookie's arm, "his vital signs seem good. His breathing and heartbeat are steady." Then more tenderly she said, "I'm afraid there isn't much more to do for such a little fellow than to watch and wait."

Watch and wait was all Sookie did. It was hard to see Sookie hover over Buddy's cage in such a worried state. Buddy's wheel stayed still and silent while the hamster lay sleeping.

Sookie never left his side, not even when the cold snap broke Saturday, much to the relief of everyone in the town. Sookie refused to go out and play – not even on Saturday afternoon when the sun was out and the temperatures turned balmy for the early days of December. Although I was worried about Buddy as well, I also had other things on my mind.

Saturday after soccer practice, I sweated in my winter jacket, and the defrosting ground sucked at my boots, almost pulling my left boot off completely. Hamster worries aside, I couldn't help but babble with Emily about the soccer match on Monday. We didn't hang out together usually, but we were discussing soccer strategies. I told her about the boys playing too hard in the gym and how we could use their wild shots to our advantage.

"I think you're right, Cat. We have a good chance to win this match and go on to the intramurals, and it feels great playing soccer again." Then Emily said, "But I'm thinking our team needs to make a change. Maybe you should be the captain of the team. You're the one who cares the most about soccer. You're the best player. Besides, I'm making a ton of money babysitting, and I don't have time to go to every practice if we make the intramurals."

I tried to think of something to say – about how, no, Emily was skilled and extra-disciplined – but I couldn't get the words out of my mouth. I was too busy basking in the warm glow of her praise. Excitement swirled inside me like a magic elixir. At least I managed to keep a grin off my face. I wanted nothing more than to lead my team to victory on Monday.

She stopped at my yard and frowned. "Hey, is your sister going to have another magic show again soon? Those two girls I babysit are always pestering me and driving me nuts."

I wanted to give her good news, especially after her generous offer of me becoming team captain, but Sookie was adamant. The Queen of Mystery was receiving no visitors while she mourned the sickness of her hamster.

I explained to Emily about Buddy. "Besides not waking up, he's not drinking or eating. But weirdly, he looks as though he's only sleeping."

"You know," Emily said thoughtfully, "maybe it has something to do with the freezing weather."

"Um, it's not freezing now," I pointed out.

"I know," Emily said with a touch of impatience, "but it was for a couple of weeks. And Buddy has ... I dunno ... hamster instincts. Maybe he decided it was time to hibernate."

Of course, that explained everything! I couldn't wait to tell Sookie.

I said bye to Emily and rushed home. I flew into the house and as usual, Sookie was in the kitchen. She hardly ever left Buddy's cage. "Sookie!" I practically shouted as I told her Emily's theory.

"That's got to be it!" Sookie eagerly agreed. "He's just in a very deep sleep. And animals don't eat anything when they hibernate, do they, Cat?"

"Nope, they live off their fat. And Buddy has a lot of that," I said.

"And he probably does drink a couple of drops of water, only when we're asleep and not watching him," Sookie decided.

I wasn't sure, but I readily agreed. I was convinced Emily had stumbled on Buddy's malady. "He's just hibernating."

A smile of relief broke over Sookie's face. "I'll go put him back in my room so we don't bother him with our voices," she whispered.

I felt quite grown up solving my sister's crisis.

That should have been a warning – sometimes a grown-up misses things and it takes a kid to see past the usual logical explanations ... at least that's my excuse.

CHAPTER 10

A Quick-Change Disaster

MONDAY MORNING WHEN Sookie came downstairs, she was once again lugging around her turban and magic box.

"I think I'll call Skeeter so we can start practicing a new magic trick after school."

"Not today," I reminded her. "Aren't you coming with Mom to my big soccer game?"

Sookie blushed. "I forgot," she said as she smiled.

"I don't know how anyone could forget the match," said Mom. "Cat's done nothing but fret about it all weekend."

"Have not," I said in surprise. I was feeling totally confident.

"Oh," said Sookie, "so we don't hear you mumbling in your sleep about how you have to beat the 'stupid boys'?"

Now it was my turn to blush while they laughed. The sun streamed through the kitchen window, lighting up the blue curtains and making them as vivid as robin's eggs. Mom stirred oatmeal and I made toast.

It was as if we'd had beautiful weather all along. And Sookie's new happy mood made it seem as if we hadn't been living under the shadow of a family tragedy. She'd come to accept Buddy's strange behavior. He still slept away, but he hadn't become any worse. He really did seem to be hibernating.

"Can we have eggs?" I asked. "I'll need the protein for the game."

"One step ahead of you," said Mom as she pointed to an egg in a pot of boiling water.

After breakfast, I packed my soccer boots into my bag, but my fingers lingered over the Grimoire soccer uniform in my drawer. How dazzling that uniform was compared to the plain yellow and red striped shirt and boring white shorts I had to wear for Darkmont's game. The green and black Grimoire uniform felt smooth to my touch, although it was as if my fingers ached to touch something else soft and silky. I couldn't quite figure out what, so I shrugged my shoulders, balled up my soccer socks, threw them in the bag, and raced out of the house for school.

"Wait up!" called Sookie who was quickly untangling the thick scarf around her neck. "It's too hot for this," she complained, stuffing the scarf through the mail slot.

We hurried along, and after I dropped Sookie off at her school, I found myself arriving at Darkmont a bit early for once. No one was hanging out at the lockers, so I decided to go to the gym and drop off my gear in the girls' changing room. A small group of kids had gathered in front of the gym door. Something about the scene made me freeze in my tracks. Amarjeet, who'd been part of the group, spotted me and rushed over. She looked worried.

"They've moved the location of the soccer match," she said breathlessly.

"What?" I squeaked. "Where?" I don't know why I said that – it wasn't as if Darkmont had another gym or anything.

"Outside on the soccer field, where do you think?" Amarjeet snapped. She was no more pleased than I was that the boys would have the bigger field to play on. That would be to their benefit because of their stamina, and they wouldn't have to struggle holding back their shots. What was to their benefit worked against us.

But I swallowed my worries and said as loud as I could manage, "No problem – we're still going to win." Amarjeet looked relieved, but then again, she couldn't hear how hard my heart was pounding. And she couldn't see Clive's face behind her. He'd just read the sign on the door, and a self-satisfied grin spread over his entire face.

I couldn't concentrate in class all day. Trust Mr. Morrows to hit us with another pop quiz – how could he do this on the day of the match? And trust Clive to sit right beside me so when we had to pass our quizzes to the next student to correct, I was supposed to swap my quiz with him. However, when the time came, it was as if the test refused to leave my fingers.

"Is there a problem, Caitlin?" Mr. Morrows asked.

I hated when teachers used my real name. Come to think of it, even when Mom said "Caitlin," it usually meant I was in trouble. Reluctantly, I passed the quiz to Clive.

"Hmm," Clive whispered. "Looks like you didn't do so well here. Too bad the quiz isn't about women scientists," he said as he sneered.

"Or magicians' assistants," I shot back. That was Clive's Achilles' heel. He hated that his little brother played second billing my sister in their magic act. Clive had such an ego. Of course, maybe I shouldn't have baited him. Now there weren't going to be any mercy marks coming my way on the quiz.

After several more torturous school hours, I finally sat in the dressing room and laced up my soccer boots. Then I joined my team and jogged onto the field and into the glorious sunshine. I would have given anything to trade the sunlight for the flickering fluorescent lights of Darkmont's drab gray gym. Still, the outside air energized me and I was ready to play. For the next little while I had only one thing on my mind – wanting the ball more than anything else.

Emily, Amarjeet, and I set up our play as Mia kicked a long shot. But when it was my turn to tap the ball back to Emily, Clive raced between us. I expected him to take off with the ball, but instead he kicked it to Jasper who scored a goal. I'd just been fooled – those two guys knew our setup. I acted as if I hadn't caught on and decided to set up my own sucker trick. The next time Mia kicked the ball to Emily, and then she kicked it to me, when Clive got ready to scoop the ball and Jasper blocked Emily, I head-butted the ball back to Mia. She was surprised, but she kicked a long shot as I raced across the field and managed to tap the ball into the goal. Over the clamor of the crowd, I could hear Sookie cheering me on.

People might think watching a close game is exciting, but playing in a close game is a lot of stress. At half-time the score was still one - one.

As we sat on the bench, Ms. Dreeble rallied us. "You girls are playing marvelously." Then she squeezed my shoulder. "And you're playing with all your heart, Cat."

Me? Did Ms. Dreeble mean me? I looked up. She seemed so serious when she said, "Putting your whole heart into something is what counts." Then she smiled and said, "Those are great qualities for a new team captain."

Suddenly some of my aches and pains faded, and I surveyed the soccer field with the eye of a team captain.

The whistle blew and we were back on the field. It was as if I already was captain. Organizing my team renewed my strength. Emily tapped the ball to me. I kept tight control. But Clive stretched out his long legs and scooped the ball. I finally understood what Mr. Morrows' meant when he said "wars were lost by attrition." The gradual wearing down of our energy would go on and on until one team finally scored.

I just couldn't let it be the boys.

When the whistle shrilled announcing the end of the game, we had managed to hang on to our one - one tie. Now there was going to be a shoot-out. Suddenly, the determination I'd felt throughout the game wavered. Endurance – Jasper had said – was the boys' advantage. We'd played long and hard until we were spent. Practicing in the gym had only backfired for the girls. We hadn't built up our stamina. Then I swallowed the butterflies that were trying to crawl out of my stomach and up my closing throat. This was no time to lose heart.

We all held our breath as Emily kicked the first ball and it sailed fast and low into the goal net! She scored and we all roared in delight. Then it was Zach's turn. He kicked hard and the ball soared high – poor Amarjeet didn't stand a chance. The boys cheered. Then it was Mia's turn. She aimed for the goalie's shoulder and slipped the ball past him and into the goal. The crowd screamed, and I think I could hear Sookie and Mom's cheers among them. Then Clive in his typical arrogant fashion barely tapped the ball and put a bend on it so it practically sailed in a circle around Amarjeet before dropping behind her and into the net. The boys jumped up and down, shouting and pounding each other on the back.

It was my turn. We were doing well – matching the boys every inch of the way. Time to show which team was superior. I marched up to the ball. But I suddenly wondered how long I could keep this up, and then my leg began to cramp. No, not now! I shouted to myself. Focus – picture where you want the ball to land. Taking a calming breath, I rubbed my leg and waited until I managed to hear even the crumpling of a soda can in the stands. Uber-focussed, I lifted my leg to kick. There was a sudden shout from the sidelines. During that split second, Clive had shoved Mitch, and Mitch yelled as he fell onto a net of soccer balls. I stumbled. The ball caught the end of my foot and instead of soaring over the field as I'd planned, the soccer ball shot up and then dropped suddenly, making an easy catch for the goalie.

Silence descended over the field as if the whole world held its breath. I couldn't believe it. At the last second I got distracted and it cost us. "Please," I pleaded under my breath, "it won't happen again. Let Jasper miss the next ball, and I promise I will never lose focus again."

Jasper approached the ball. He kicked. The ball soared and landed neatly inside the goal right behind Amarjeet. The boys won!

I stared at the boys in disbelief as they carried Jasper off the field.

Jasper, my nerdy neighbor – my one-time friend – was finally cool.

And I was the girl who lost the soccer match.

The girl who cost our team the intramurals.

CHAPTER 11

A Not So Grand Finale

I SLINKED BACK to my team, wishing *I* could somehow crawl into Sookie's purple turban and disappear. Everyone avoided me. I mean, what could my friends do? They were disappointed. Hey, it didn't even matter. No one could be more disgusted with me than I was. Huddling behind the chain-link fence, I watched as the boys finally stopped cheering and then gathered in a circle, pounding each other on the back. My own team began to form a line, and as I watched from the sidelines, the two teams streamed across the field shaking each others' hands.

What was astonishing was how the girls were laughing and joking with the guys as they shook hands. Weren't they devastated? It was as if I was far removed from the whole scene, a tiny insect on a leaf watching the mini dramas. When Mitch walked by Mia, his hand barely grazed her fingers. I could tell by Mia's frown that she was disappointed. But when Jasper and Mia met up, he held his hand out and she didn't even give him any eye contact. Her head was down, and she rushed past as if *he* was an insect on a leaf. Oddly, I noticed Emily made sure her hand lingered a lot longer in Clive's hand than in Zach's. But my short escape into the mini soap opera of Darkmont High abruptly ended with Ms. Dreeble's sharp reprimand.

"Cat, I don't know you all that well, but I'm surprised by your utterly poor sportsmanship. Get out on that field and shake hands with the winning team."

Her anger shocked me, but I was more shocked at myself. She was right. I had my dignity, and that meant that even though I lost for the girls' team, I had to hold my head up and shake the guys' hands. Hurrying to get it over with, I dashed to the field and held out my hand.

"You played impressively through the whole game," Jasper said. "It wasn't your fault Mitch squirted Clive in the face with a water bottle, just when you were about to kick the ball." Jasper gripped my hand and gave it a firm shake. What he described wasn't what I'd seen. I thought Clive had sabotaged me.

"Good game," Zach said to me, as if he was reciting the periodic table in science class. But then he stopped and said, "Really, you're a great player. The girls' team was awesome."

That was generous. I blinked hard to stop my eyes from stinging. Even Mitch, who was trying to trip some of the guys ahead of us, managed a brief smile and a sincere, "Good game."

When it was Clive's turn, my heart sank to my soccer boots as he swaggered toward me. "What did I tell you," he said. "You are ..."

What – not as good as boys? I lost it.

Seriously.

Instead of shaking his hand, I stuck my tongue out and quickly turned away. He looked surprised, but he just shrugged. There was a shrill blast of the whistle to get our attention. Mr. Morrows and Ms. Dreeble stood in the middle of the soccer field.

"It has come to my attention that there was some kind of contest between the boys and girls over this match – something about the intramurals," announced Mr. Morrows in his loud teacher-voice. "I don't know who came up with that ridiculous idea."

A bunch of kids began to talk all at once. Fortunately, there was such a rumpus that the teachers probably didn't hear my name repeated the most. Meanwhile, I tried to make myself invisible by ducking behind the goal net.

"The students don't decide who is eligible for the soccer intramurals. The teaching staff at Darkmont makes that decision. I need you all to listen!" Our history teacher bellowed over the clamor.

A hush finally fell over the boys' and girls' teams.

"Both soccer teams are outstanding. Both teams will be going to the intramurals," Ms. Dreeble announced.

There was a roar of cheers and shouts, and parents on the benches clapped. My spirits lifted higher, as if I had actually scored that last goal – well almost. We could all play soccer, and those boys had better watch out, because the girls' team would bring back the intramural cup. We would kick their ...

"How can Darkmont afford to sponsor both teams?" a voice rang out from the crowd – a voice that made me flinch. It was Clive, of course.

"Well," Mr. Morrows cleared his throat. "That will be a challenge."

The boys began to mumble.

"However," said Ms. Dreeble. "We are currently looking into fundraising options. We'll keep you posted."

Then a few parents began to murmur. But it didn't matter – the girls were going to the intramurals! I floated off the field.

"Caitlin Peters," a cold voice summoned.

There was that full version of my name again. Slowly, I turned. Ms. Dreeble stood in front of me with her arms crossed and a frown that managed to include her mouth, her eyes, and even her eyeglasses. I gulped.

"I saw you stick out your tongue at Clive. We cannot have a team captain who is also a poor sport," Ms. Dreeble scolded. "I've asked Emily to remain as team captain, and in light of her having less time for those duties, I've decided you will assist her."

"In what way?" I managed to utter. It felt as if a soccer ball had just hit me in the stomach.

Ms. Dreeble adjusted her glasses on her nose and tightened the elastic on her blond ponytail. "Your duties will be to arrive early for every game and set up the soccer nets. You will also stay late for every game, take down the net, and gather all the balls. You will do this for the boys' team as well. Be prepared to do this Monday through Thursday. And on Friday, you will be responsible for gathering the soccer jerseys, laundering them, and returning them to school neatly pressed for Monday morning."

What? Although I simply nodded, my ears rang from all the screaming inside my head of how unfair this was.

"And for the future, the slightest display of poor sportsmanship will result in you being benched." Ms. Dreeble leaned toward me. "Have I made myself clear?"

Clear as a frozen night where the stars and moon glared cold and cruel. "Yes." I nodded again, this time because my voice sounded all crumpled.

Then Ms. Dreeble spun around on her gleaming white sneakers and strode away without looking back at me once. A low whistle sounded behind me. I turned. Clive had heard the whole thing. I stormed away before he could say a word.

I'd learned my lesson. There was something about Clive that destroyed my judgment. It was for the best if I stayed away from him completely.

For the next week, I worked extra hard. This improved my relationship with Ms. Dreeble somewhat; she grudgingly acknowledged I'd showed up every day before and after school to take care of the nets. Also, Monday morning the soccer jerseys arrived clean and pressed. That week I played the best soccer ever, and even Ms. Dreeble was forced to comment on my skills. For bonus points, I handed all my science homework in early. I figured it wouldn't hurt. Maybe Ms. Dreeble would be so happy with my perfect behavior, she would relent and allow me to take my rightful place as team captain. I had to hang on to that hope.

Yes, I was turning things around.

If only there hadn't been a new competition starting, I could have stayed away from Clive.

... and a world of trouble!

CHAPTER 12

The Magic Darkens

"**WE'VE ORGANIZED A** fundraiser for the intra-murals, and I'd like you to help, Cat."

Ms. Dreeble was the first one to mention Sookie's school and its winterfest pageant. She had figured out even more work I could do on behalf of our soccer program.

I nodded wearily, as it had been a long day beginning with an extra-early morning because I'd left washing the soccer jerseys until the last minute. That was followed by net setup, a load of schoolwork, and soccer practice after school. Now I was stuffing the last soccer ball into the gym utility closet.

"What would you like me to do?" I asked Ms. Dreeble as politely as I could.

"I need you to pitch in and help out with the Drearden talent show."

"Drearden's what?" I asked.

"Drearden Elementary School is having a pageant on December 19th, the day before winter break. Instead of the usual holiday sing, the school is inviting the elementary school children to hold a talent contest."

Why is this supposed to include me, I thought, but I didn't ask. Not that I needed to ask, because Ms. Dreeble happily ticked off her expectations on her fingers.

"One – our soccer teams will help out by selling tickets, and two – the show will be held in our gym because we have the biggest stage. Three – we'll set up the concert chairs, four – we'll provide refreshments and we'll sell baked goods. Five ..." a satisfied smile spread across Ms. Dreeble's face as she ticked off the last point on her pinky finger, "the elementary school will split all the proceeds with us in exchange."

I guess she thought this was an easy way to raise money for the intramural costs without bothering our parents. Every kid knows parents love school concerts.

"So I can count on you, Cat, for supervising ticket sales, the bake sale, and the setup and take down of equipment."

Ms. Dreeble hadn't exactly asked; she simply assumed. She didn't even wait for my answer as she raced back to her classroom. I finished tucking the last soccer ball on the shelf and gathered up my coat, scarf, and gloves – after the soccer match, the weather turned cold again. As I stepped carefully along the ice-covered sidewalks and crunched through a field of frozen grass, I grimly wondered how to squeeze these new talent show duties into my already-tight schedule. Plus, I'd have to hang around the whole evening of the talent show and watch a boring contest, which I was sure would be pretty sad. I could already picture the clunky tap dancing and screeching instruments. With a shudder, I slowly climbed the steps to my front porch, opened the door, and walked into the heat.

Sookie squealed a quick hello while she danced up and down in the living room, unable to contain her glee. "Do you know what, Cat?" Her face dimpled and her eyes widened with excitement.

"Let me guess," I said with a less than enthusiastic sigh. "Your magic act is going public. The Queen of Mystery is about to gain a bigger audience."

Sookie gasped in surprise. "How do you know?"

"You're looking at your roadie," I sighed again.

"What does that mean?"

"A roadie is a person who does all the grunt work, setting up and taking down equipment for an event." I did a little bow. "That will be me, the force behind the Drearden talent contest."

Sookie said, "Oh, I'm sorry, Cat. That doesn't sound very fun."

"Hey, it's probably for the best." I slumped in the wingback chair. I'd started getting into the idea that my sister could probably win the talent contest. All the kids loved her magic act. And I could help her. I mean, I wouldn't go as far as being her new assistant or anything, but I could help her set up and learn new tricks.

"I'll do extra work for your magic act, Sookie. You're the talented one in the family. This will be your time to shine."

"You're talented," argued Sookie.

"Are you kidding?" I laughed. "Except for playing soccer, I can't dance, or sing, or paint, or even hold a poem in my head for more than one minute. Like I said, you're the talented one." The phone rang at that moment. Sookie usually raced to answer it, but now she didn't budge.

"Cat," she said earnestly, "don't you understand you have a very special talent?"

"And that would be ... " I was feeling less like joking now. I had a ton of homework, and I wanted to do well in my ongoing campaign to convince Ms. Dreeble I had reformed and was now truly a good sport – and an aspiring good student.

"Sookie," Mom called from the kitchen. "It's Skeeter."

That was too much temptation for Sookie. She ran off to answer the phone. Mom wandered into the living room, asking how my day was.

"Great," I said, like always.

A tiny frown tugged the corners of her mouth. "These days, Cat, you never have much to tell me. You know I'm interested in what's going on in your life."

I understood she wanted more detail. But what could I say? Well, Mom, in addition to working off the biggest detention I've ever had, my teacher has found a new way to torture me with additional work. I'll never get to be captain of my soccer team, or be as popular as I was in my old town. Oh, and if I mess up once, I may not be able to play in the intramurals.

Instead I said, "Really great."

Mom shook her head. She looked as if she was about to say something else, but just then our furnace let out a little burp, then a chug, and then a loud bang, as if someone had lit a firecracker in the basement. The curtains that had been fluttering steadily with the blow of constant heat suddenly wilted. Immediately a chilling draft swept across the room.

"Oh no." Mom's face crumpled. "Our furnace can't give out now – not in this freezing cold weather."

She didn't know it, but at night when I came downstairs for a glass of water, I could see her hunched over her desk, fretting over the bills. Last week she'd muttered out loud over our gas bill being "twice as high" as she'd expected because of the "bizarre winter weather." I knew there was no way we could afford furnace repairs on top of everything else.

"Grab a flashlight, Cat." Mom rushed toward the furnace room, which was in the cellar.

I reminded myself that I'm not afraid of the dark. But I'm not a big fan of it, or of damp, creepy places underground where spiders, or mice, or nasty secret things lurked – especially since I'd had to go down a stone staircase once – deep underground. I'd seen things then that still haunted my dreams. Dark, damp, and creepy – that was basically our cellar. I dug the flashlight out of the closet and followed my mom down the rickety stairs under the back porch. I should have put my jacket on, or at least my scarf, as the cold wind stabbed through my shirt and made my ears ache.

At the bottom of the stairs, Mom pulled the chain on the lightbulb that dangled from the ceiling. With a click of the chain, the inky black faded to the corners of the cellar, and a weak yellow light beamed down. I aimed the flashlight at the far wall, and Mom got to work, checking the pilot light.

"Cat, I need you to aim the flashlight right here below the furnace. I have to re-light the pilot. A draft must have blown it out."

While we were down there, I used the flashlight to check out the heating ducts. I remembered that I had thought Sookie and Skeeter had shoved things down the heat register when the audience wasn't looking and I was sure that's how they made things disappear. But there were no signs of broken egg shell or a coin. Still there had to be a logical explanation for why my sister was so good at making things disappear – right?

"Cat, I need the light over here."

I directed the flashlight while Mom relit the furnace. With a big gush of air, the furnace suddenly began to chug away, and Mom's relief was clear, even in the dim shadows of the cellar. But I thought the furnace still didn't sound very healthy.

When Mom and I got back to the kitchen, Sookie was crying at the table.

"What's wrong? Has something happened to Buddy?" I asked.

"No, he's still hibernating." Sookie sniffed. "I'm upset because Skeeter just phoned to tell me he can't be my assistant anymore."

"Oh? Why not?" asked Mom in the cheery voice she often used to calm things down.

"Because he says he has to be in a rock band for Drearden's talent contest. His brother is making him play with sixth- and seventh-graders who have a really cool band. Clive told them Skeeter was a great guitar player."

Everyone who watches TV knows that rock groups always win the talent contest. Plus, for the first time, I considered that Sookie's magic act required close-up attention from her audience. In a small room my sister made it look as if objects were disappearing. It was hard to see how Sookie would manage that kind of trick with an adult audience sitting farther away from a big stage. And she used such tiny props like eggs and coins; no one would see that. Besides, it would be especially difficult for her quiet act to compete with a rock band.

It was one thing for Clive to ruin my success. There was no way I could let him wreck Sookie's time to shine. My sister was going to win the Drearden contest.

I was going to help any way I could.

CHAPTER 13

Conjuring Trouble

SOOKIE WAS GOING to have to pull off an amazing illusion for the talent show. I went to the computer and Googled "Magic Tricks for Kids" and printed off a bunch of pages.

"Check this out," I said with enthusiasm as I handed her the sheets. Sookie shuffled through the paper, but she didn't seem as excited as I was.

"Are you ready to roll up your sleeves and get to work?" I encouraged her. Funny, it was much easier to be an overachiever on my sister's behalf.

"Cat, I already have an idea for a great trick."

So Sookie didn't need my help. Maybe that was for the best because some of the tricks I'd printed out looked kind of difficult. I had no idea how my sister, who was just a little kid, managed to pull off her illusions. Clearly magic wasn't my talent. But I felt I knew what it took to win, so I gave her advice anyway.

"Make sure it's a mind-blowing trick. It's got to look good in front of a large audience. A disappearing egg won't cut it this time. You have to go for a big illusion that will show up well on a stage."

"My idea will be impressive, Cat. It's just that – "

"Don't get discouraged – you can do it." I tried saying what Mom might tell her.

Then getting completely off topic, Sookie said, "It's

a really bad winter. Buddy will have to keep hibernating, won't he?"

I shrugged my shoulders, wanting to get back to coaching Sookie's magic act so she'd blast Clive's – I mean, Skeeter's – rock group off the stage. "Sure, that makes sense – he'll sleep through all this cold weather."

"That's the only reason he's still asleep, right, Cat?"

Why was Sookie suddenly concerned about Buddy again? We'd kept a close watch on her hamster. He didn't wake up, but he wasn't getting worse. I thought she'd accepted his condition.

"Yes. He's hibernating." I said this firmly so my sister would get back on track. There's no winning without completely focusing on the goal.

Sookie let her breath out between her teeth, almost hissing like a cat. "Okay. I'll do it."

"Do what? What trick are you going to do?"

"Conjuring," Sookie said with a sly smile.

"Conjuring what?"

"That's a magician's secret." My sister wouldn't say another word to me.

Instead, she called up a few of her classmates and asked if they were interested in auditioning to be her new assistant. Sookie wasn't about to pine for Skeeter, although she clearly missed him. All the kids she phoned were excited about trying out for the assistant's position.

On Sunday afternoon, I hung out behind the kitchen door and listened to Sookie interview prospective apprentices in person. She'd ask them all the same question: "Are you good at keeping secrets?"

When it was Raj's turn, he said, "I keep lots of secrets. Just ask my sister." Amarjeet, who had been listening with me, frowned in a way that made me think Raj had a gift for blackmail.

Sookie hesitated before she handed Raj the shirt and bow tie that Skeeter always wore. Raj didn't seem to notice her reluctance – he was grinning from ear to ear.

***

When Sookie didn't want my help in learning new illusions, I found a different way to help her. For one thing, I used my position as the roadie for the Drearden talent contest to get permission for Sookie to move the old trunk up onto the stage at our school. She insisted she needed it there to practice her surprise magic trick. I also made sure my sister got the most rehearsal time of all the elementary school acts. I also placed her show last on the program. The audience voted for the winner, and everyone knows that people always remember the last event best.

On a Friday afternoon, the week before our Christmas break – and most importantly, the week before the talent show – Mom, Sookie, and I loaded the magician's trunk into our car. We folded down the backseat to make room for Sookie's props, and then Mom drove to the school. I had to walk to Darkmont to meet up with them, as there was only room left for two passengers in the car.

I hoped my family appreciated that I was almost frozen to death by the time I joined them in the gym. Winter weather was still hitting our town hard. We'd had a heap of snow. Actually, the whole town looked very Christmassy with the weather, and you couldn't help but get excited for the holiday. Except that we were behind on our Christmas shopping because the one highway leading out of town was barely letting traffic through, and Mom hated driving in the snow. The river that surrounded the town had frozen, although none of our parents were allowing us to skate on it yet. Grim Hill looked like a regular snow-capped alpine mountain. But no one seemed interested in tobogganing there, even though it was the only big hill in town.

Once inside the gym, I rubbed my legs, trying to make the numbing chill disappear. Sookie had met up with Jasper and Zach who had been hanging out in the gym shooting hoops. They were now helping her and Mom with the trunk. As I climbed up on the stage, Jasper and Zach were setting the trunk upright. The blue cape that Sookie had decorated with silver moons and stars hung across the top of the trunk like a curtain. Jasper parted the curtain and checked inside.

"Out, out," Sookie said as she shooed Jasper away.

Reluctantly, Jasper closed the curtain. While Sookie got to work directing Zach and Mom on turning the cabinet slightly to the left, then to the right, then back again, Jasper pulled me off center stage and behind a heavy curtain.

"What's Sookie up to now?" he asked in a worried voice.

"It's a secret."

"But you know what the secret is, right?" Jasper was frowning.

"Of course ..." But I think he saw through to the truth – the fact that I had no idea.

Jasper shook his head and mumbled, "You understand the difference between illusion and real magic, don't you?"

"Why wouldn't I? You explained it once or twice."

"What I mean is, you're keeping a close eye on your sister, aren't you? You're watching out ..."

I was about to ask "Watching out for what?" but Amarjeet arrived with Raj, and my sister was ready to begin rehearsals. Sookie demanded the boys get off the stage, and then I ran to the wall and pulled the ropes, closing the stage curtains. Sookie made it clear rehearsal had to be done in private. Still, I was pretty surprised when Sookie pushed me away too.

Mom left me in charge as she rushed back to the office to finish her photocopying for all the teachers. Amarjeet and I hung around the gym with Jasper and Zach. We took the second basketball and shot a few hoops, but I almost wanted to jump through the hoop myself, and ask Zach, "So, do you notice me now?"

Couldn't he tell Emily was more interested in that jerk Clive?

I wasn't the only one distracted. Jasper kept looking toward the stage. He'd jump at every little sound. After a clang and bump behind the curtain, he raced toward the stage; I ran after him and shouted, "Sookie, is everything all right?"

"Yes, everything is going great," she called back.

Jasper walked away with me, but he kept looking back at the stage.

After that, our shooting hoops fell apart and Zach left. Amarjeet sat down on the bench waiting for Sookie and Raj to finish, while I made sure Jasper didn't try to spy on my sister by pacing back and forth in front of the stage. I wasn't about to let him run to Clive with any secrets ever again, although Jasper maintained he'd never done that in the first place.

When my Mom arrived to pick us up, she offered to take us all for strawberry tapioca tea at the nearby Bubble Tea Palace, but Raj dozed off in the car. Mom drove Raj and his sister home instead. I asked Sookie how she managed to wear him out with the preparation for her trick.

She only told me it was a secret.

CHAPTER 14

A Mysterious Malady

RAJ WAS SICK the very next day after rehearsal, and his mother called to say he would not be able to be a magician's assistant for the Queen of Mystery. Sookie had to recruit another assistant, and then another, and still another. But each time the new assistant showed up for the magic rehearsal, the next day, that kid was sick. Even though students from her class were lining up to volunteer for her, there was a bad flu going through Sookie's school, and pretty soon she was running out of assistants. Fortunately, the older grades hadn't gotten the bug yet. Sookie was fine though – not even a sore throat – but the flu was causing a big headache for her magic act.

Then Sookie's latest assistant, Mia's sister Toni, became ill. One by one, all the kids from her class who wanted to be her assistant caught the flu. Mostly I'd stayed out of the magic act though, as Sookie was managing fine by herself. I was busy at soccer practice, getting ready for the intramurals.

The afternoon before the talent show, and two days before the intramurals, Sookie was training a new girl named Anne. She was assistant number ten by my count.

That day, while Sookie was up on the stage rehearsing, I was setting up the gym for the talent contest, along with players from both the girls' and boys' soccer teams. We'd decorated everything with red and green streamers and balloons. The elementary school provided us with tons of white paper snowflakes, which took us forever to tape onto the walls. They'd also made red and green paper lanterns, which were a pain in the neck to hang along the stage, but I knew the kids would be checking to make sure that we'd used all their decorations. Finally, we arranged the chairs. There were two hundred seats to set up! This was a small town and not too many exciting things happened – no fancy plays or concerts. This talent contest was sure to be a big hit with the parents and all the people in town.

Ms. Dreeble arrived after most of the other kids had left. I was still arranging the green paper programs on the seats of the chairs.

"Cat, this gym looks great!" she said.

I wanted her to say that since I'd worked so hard I should automatically be team captain.

"We've definitely raised enough money for the intramurals," she said. "Are you ready for our game?"

It wasn't exactly the heaps of praise I was looking for, but I couldn't fault my teacher for keeping her soccer focus. That mattered a lot to me, too, and I couldn't wait for the game. Not to mention that all this volunteering also went along nicely with me helping Sookie win the talent contest. I nodded and tried looking dedicated and exhausted at the same time as I placed another program on a chair.

"You know," said Ms. Dreeble, "Emily is still interested in stepping down as captain of the girls' soccer team. She's apparently babysitting quite a lot."

My heart started banging loudly enough to echo in my ears. I almost grinned, but I made my face freeze because Ms. Dreeble hadn't yet said anything specific.

"I'm thinking maybe it would be better if we had the new team captain begin with the first game. Are you still interested, Cat?"

"Yes." I swallowed hard. It's funny. When something so important – something that you've been looking forward to so much – happens, it's as if your mind blanks out. The best I could come up with was one word. And I didn't even sound all that excited.

Ms. Dreeble looked as if she'd been expecting more of an outburst from me. Usually she was trying to get me to behave the opposite way. But she said, "Good, then it's settled."

Team captain! I finished the rest of the setup for the show, told some of my friends the good news, and then rushed home to tell Sookie and Mom.

Dinner that night was my favorite: chili with garlic bread on the side, a perfect celebration for a great day. I was team captain! And my sister would win Drearden's talent contest. I could finally put Clive in his place.

***

"Hurry up or we'll be late," commanded the Queen of Mystery.

Thursday evening, Sookie stood at the top of our staircase. She was dressed for her magic show in black jeans, a crisp white blouse, black jacket, red cape, and of course, the turban. Mom had pointed out Sookie might trip over the sparkly red gown she'd discovered in the old trunk, but my sister refused to give up the purple turban. I had to admit, she did look like a magician – ridiculous hat or not.

Sookie didn't look one bit nervous, but I had enough butterflies crashing around in my stomach for both of us. We bundled up in scarves, hats, gloves, and thick jackets. The road was icy, but Mom had broken down and bought snow tires, complaining about how she'd never expected that kind of expense.

Personally, I was feeling very lucky. Now I was captain of the soccer team; there was an exciting game tomorrow, and both the boys and girls would be playing in it. Ticket sales for the contest were staggering, which meant there would be money left over for dinner in the city tomorrow night for all the players after the game. It just didn't get better than that. And my sister was about to kick serious butt with her magic show tonight. Poor Clive and Skeeter.

When we pulled into the high school, we saw Jasper directing parking – not a great job to be chosen for, considering it was so cold outside. When I went through the door, Amarjeet grabbed me and asked me to help her sell last-minute tickets, even though that hadn't been one of my jobs. She was biting her lip, and she rubbed her head as if it ached.

"I'm sorry," she whispered. "But I have to get home." Her voice caught and it sounded as if she was trying not to cry. "My brother has been in a coma. I'm going to the hospital tonight to visit him."

Alarmed I said, "I'm so sorry. I didn't know."

"I guess he's going to be okay," Amarjeet said as if she was trying to convince herself. "The doctors say all his vital signs are good."

I didn't know what to say. I told her that I hoped he would be all right, but it just didn't seem like enough. I took the ticket envelope and replaced Amarjeet at the front door. She raced off looking extremely worried.

Within minutes, it got really busy. Townspeople streamed in as I collected all the tickets and pointed everyone to the gym. The show was about to begin.

When the lights dimmed, I ran across the hall to the

lunchroom and double-checked that coffee, tea, and hot apple cider would be ready to go at intermission. I also helped Mia put out the baked goods we'd be selling. She seemed distracted and she almost tipped over a tray of cupcakes that were piled high with chocolate and vanilla frosting.

"Watch out," I said, grabbing the tray.

"Oh. Sorry ..." Together we carefully placed the tray on a cafeteria table. Then she sat down with a sigh. "This just isn't as much fun when my own sister can't be here. Toni was so looking forward to the magic show, and she was super-excited that Sookie had chosen her as an assistant."

"How's she feeling?" I asked.

"Lately she just sleeps," said Mia.

The hair on the back of my neck tingled, and I felt goose bumps break out on my arms. My mind was turning. Sleeping ... that was Raj's problem too. Come to think of it, that was also Buddy's problem. Was this all a coincidence? No big deal, I tried to convince myself, except coincidences were generally not a good thing in this town ...

Just then I heard shouting outside in the hallway.

CHAPTER 15

The Last Assistant

"**YOU CAN'T BACK** out now!" Clive yelled at his brother. "You're the lead guitarist."

Skeeter simply shook his head. "I quit. All Sookie's magician's assistants are sick. She needs me."

Again I got a different opinion of Skeeter. I had thought he was a sellout, abandoning Sookie just because his brother said he should. But when the two brothers stood together in the hall, I could see that Clive was quite a force. He was tall for his age and lots taller than Skeeter. He also looked really, really angry. But Skeeter quietly stood up to him. He slipped the electric guitar strap off his shoulder and handed the guitar to his older brother. Clive snatched it out of his hands.

"You're letting your group down." Clive shook his head.

"They don't need me. Sookie does."

No one else in the rock band seemed that upset that Skeeter was backing out. I wondered why. Then a freckle-faced kid with a mop of light brown hair and a black T-shirt said, "C'mon, Clive. This is really your band. You should be the one who plays with us tonight."

The other boys nodded. So ... Clive was the one who played in this rock group ...

"You can't let your band down," said Skeeter.

The boys all agreed. Clive strapped on the guitar and stormed off to the stage area with the rest of the band trailing behind.

Clive was going to appear on stage in front of all the kids on our soccer teams and play music with sixth- and seventh-graders – how perfect was that? I broke out into a huge grin.

"C'mon, Skeeter," I said. "I'll show you where Sookie is."

"You mean, the Queen of Mystery. We'd better hurry."

I brought Skeeter backstage. By the way she hugged him, I assumed Sookie was ecstatic to take Skeeter back on with such late notice – not that she had much choice. Anne didn't show up tonight. She was sick. It was lucky Sookie hadn't caught the flu – or Skeeter for that matter.

Sookie helped her assistant with his bow tie.

"So what trick are we doing?" asked Skeeter.

Sookie leaned forward and whispered into Skeeter's ear.

"Awesome!" he said.

Then they shooed me off stage.

Finally, I took a seat in the gym to watch the show. Except, what was I thinking? For the next thirty minutes I endured squeaking violins, toots, and squeals from trumpets and singers so off-key my ears ached. I sat through a dance act where I nervously watched a girl trip several times and almost tumble from the stage in her enthusiasm. When it was intermission, I was happy to abandon my seat and head to the lunchroom.

I rushed around pouring coffee and tea for the adults, handing out treats, collecting money, and making change. At the end of intermission as the next act was announced, the adults hurried back to their seats. They all seemed to be enjoying the show. At the last minute, Mitch showed up at the refreshment table. I waited until Emily carried the coffee urn away before I asked him an important question – something I'd just thought of.

"Are you interested in a few freebies ... in exchange for a favor?" I asked him as I reached under the table and produced a plate stacked with cupcakes.

"What type of favor?" asked Mitch. He looked tempted.

"Some special lighting for my sister's magic act," I said, holding the plate close to his nose so he could get a good whiff of chocolate.

Mitch reached out, grabbed a cupcake, and sank his teeth into it. Then he smiled, displaying his icing-covered teeth. "I guarantee Sookie will be in the spotlight for her whole act," he said as he grabbed more cupcakes.

A few minutes later, the show began. I had to admit the second half offered some tough competition for Sookie. Two school gymnasts performed an impressive tumbling and juggling act. They could even throw hoops in the air, do cartwheels, and then catch the hoops, never stumbling on the stage. The audience roared. The gymnasts were so good, I bet that even though they were in grade six, they could get jobs with Cirque du Soleil.

Next, there was a little girl with dark hair who wore a frilly white dress. She was maybe in grade two. She played the piano better than any one I'd ever heard.

I'd done my best to make sure Sookie was last, but Clive pulled a few strings of his own and booked his band right before her.

When Clive appeared onstage, towering over those younger kids, all of us on the soccer teams burst out laughing. I could almost see a tornado of anger swirling over Clive's head like in a cartoon. But my laughter died on my lips when Clive began playing.

Clive was an astonishingly good singer and guitarist. I mean, although it disgusted me to even think it, he was talented. His band played a cover of a popular song and they sounded as good as the original band. When they finished, the audience – including all the kids on our team – thundered applause. I started to get really worried about Sookie's grand finale.

As the applause died down, the curtains closed on Clive's rock band. When the curtains swooshed open again, the gym was plunged into darkness, except for the spotlight. Mitch kept his end of the deal. He shone the yellow light right on Sookie and her magician's trunk.

I caught my breath as the audience became quiet. It was as if everyone else in the auditorium had left.

And the only thing I saw was Sookie crossing the stage stiffly, like a zombie – as if she was under some sort of magical spell herself.

CHAPTER 16

The Spirit Cabinet

SOOKIE BECKONED HER assistant. Skeeter strode toward the audience with the confidence of a star performer. He didn't look one bit nervous. Some parents in the audience broke into a few chuckles as the ridiculous turban wobbled on my sister's head. But their laughing quickly became more hesitant as Sookie's voice rang out across the stage and echoed through the gym.

"Magic is mysterious," she said in a spooky voice. "And magicians have their secrets. I am about to conjure a trick for the ages." With a flourish of her arm, Sookie pointed to the trunk. "This is a spirit cabinet. And it contains many mysteries."

The trunk was standing upright like a magician's cabinet, and draped across the front was the silver-sparkled blue curtain. Sookie pulled the curtain. Skeeter, who'd been standing to the left of the cabinet, ducked and stepped inside. Yanking the curtain closed, Sookie stepped back from her cabinet, and we couldn't even see the tips of Skeeter's red sneakers sticking out from behind the curtain.

"I will conjure the disappearance of my assistant," Sookie said in that peculiar, distant voice. "Then, I will make him reappear."

My heart fell.

How would Sookie manage such an illusion? This wasn't our living room where Skeeter could hide objects under a rug or behind a curtain when we all looked the other way. Sookie was now high up on the gym stage. And another thing: this was Skeeter she was trying to make disappear. She couldn't exactly slip him under her sleeve. I began to worry that my sister wouldn't win the talent show. That I'd – I mean – she'd be humiliated.

Then Sookie began to sing an eerie song, and it was as if an ice cube slid down my spine. I started shivering violently.

"Foo-thee-on-lan-ive!" she shouted when she finished her song.

The spirit cabinet rocked, and when Sookie whipped the curtain open ...

Skeeter wasn't there!

The audience clapped loudly – louder than they had for any other act. But I couldn't concentrate. There was a buzzing in my head as if a smoke alarm was going off in my brain, screeching "Danger!"

Turning the cabinet from front to back, the Queen of Mystery displayed that there were no hidden curtains, ropes, mirrors, or anything that would help with such a big illusion. I should have been ecstatic about my sister's success; after all, she managed to pull off an awesome trick. But all I could think of was, hurry Sookie, bring Skeeter back.

Once more, Sookie closed the curtain. Then she began singing her creepy tune again. Jasper emerged from the back of the audience, squeezed into my row, and knelt down beside my chair.

"Something is really wrong here, Cat," he wheezed.

I could hardly answer him because my throat had turned to sandpaper. But I gulped, "Wait. She said she'd bring Skeeter back."

"Th-oe-rum-on-wa-je!" Sookie called out.

Again the spirit cabinet tilted and shook. Then the whole stage shuddered, and the red and green paper lanterns above the stage swung and appeared to swirl with a ghostly white glow. Even the gym floor vibrated under my feet.

Sookie opened the curtain, and I let out a huge sigh of relief. Skeeter stepped from the spirit cabinet. "See," I said to Jasper, although the alarm bell still clanged in my head. "Everything is okay."

Skeeter began walking. Then he stumbled and fell flat on the stage.

"What happened?" people shouted as everyone rushed to the stage. "Is he hurt?"

The town doctor was in the audience and she hurried up to the stage to examine Skeeter. Her daughter, the little pianist, clung to the doctor's pant leg. "Help him, Mommy!" she cried and then she burst into tears.

The girl wasn't the only child who was upset. I stood on the stage looking behind the curtain at Sookie who had gone so pale, I thought she might faint. When I looked back at Skeeter lying lifeless on the hardwood floor of the stage, my heart lurched. Clive and an elderly woman hovered over him.

"Don't worry, Gran," Clive said in a perfectly worried voice. Then he asked people to step away from his brother while the doctor examined him.

Jasper had rushed to Sookie and put his arm around her. He was speaking quietly, and Sookie nodded. Mom came up to me and said, "I've called an ambulance."

In just a few minutes, we heard the whoop whoop of the siren. When the paramedics opened the gym door to bring in a stretcher, a brutal gust of icy wind blasted through the gym. Everyone threw on their coats and scarves. I heard the doctor speaking to Clive and his grandmother as the paramedics took Skeeter out in a stretcher. "He's unconscious, but his pulse is steady and his breathing is regular."

For some reason, all I could think of was Raj and Toni again – and even Buddy – and how they all slept on and on and on ... A cramp of worry tugged at my insides, and for a sick moment, I wondered if Skeeter would ever wake up. But of course he would ... they all would. It was just a bad flu going around, that was all.

Clive's grandmother left with the ambulance, and parents began bundling their kids and heading out the doors. That was the end of the Drearden talent contest. Nobody cared about who would win anymore. I watched Clive as he stood alone amongst the crowd, and I felt I had to say something. But what do you say to the boy you detest when a terrible thing has just happened. Slowly I walked over to him.

"Skeeter's a great kid," I said sincerely. "I just know he'll be okay." But would he? My insides cramped up again. Then Mom offered to drive Clive to the hospital. "Are you coming now, Cat?" she asked.

I looked at Jasper and he shook his head wildly. We had to talk.

"Is it okay if I walk home with Jasper?"

Mom nodded, "But don't stay too late. It's dark out and you have a long day tomorrow – with the game and then dinner in town." She led Clive and a very subdued Sookie out of the gym and to the car.

Jasper and I lingered behind, and as soon as most of the people left, we discussed the event. We were both really shaken, and despite our differences lately, he was the only one I could talk to about Grim Hill and the secrets it held – that is, without me appearing crazy.

"Jasper, I'm worried. I don't think Skeeter was the first person Sookie made disappear and reappear. As a matter of fact, I bet that was what was happening to every one of Sookie's assistants. Each time she had a rehearsal, I'm sure she was practicing making her assistant disappear. Plus, it seems every one of her friends – and even her pet – have fallen asleep right after she made them reappear."

"I think you're right," agreed Jasper. "This isn't good – there are a lot of sick kids."

"And they haven't woken up," I said as a horrible feeling now came over me. "I can't shake the idea that there is a connection. A connection to you-know-where ... Grim Hill."

"I've been trying to tell you there's something just not right about all this magic Sookie's into." Jasper slammed his fists together.

"We don't know that for sure," I said a bit defensively. But I thought about what Amarjeet had said – about being so worried for her brother who was now in the hospital. I rubbed the back of my neck. It was aching like crazy. "If kids were getting ill anyhow, and they were spending time out in this cold weather going back and forth to rehearsal, that could make them worse, right?"

"Then how come no one in our school has the flu? Or Sookie?" Jasper wondered. "Or any other kids in the elementary school? Almost everyone in town was here for the show – except the families of your sister's assistants." Jasper scratched his head and said, "I don't like where this is going – it reminds me how the fairies tried to steal children at Halloween."

"No ... not steal ... no one is missing," my words stumbled out. Every kid was accounted for – except they had a weird flu. But there was that connection to Sookie. They'd all been her assistants. And as for her incredible magic – why hadn't I noticed before? Why didn't alarms clang in my head earlier?

The last of the boys and girls from our soccer teams left the gym. When they opened the doors, the temperature, which was already cold, plunged again. Jasper and I hurried to put on our coats and scarves and then hightailed it out of there. Ms. Dreeble who was locking everything up, chased after me.

"Cat, your sister left this on the stage." Ms. Dreeble handed over Sookie's turban as if she couldn't wait to get rid of it.

I stared at the purple turban with the black feather sticking out of the glittering ruby brooch. Automatically my fingers stretched out and stroked the silky plume. But that feather didn't feel silky at all – not like another feather that I was starting to remember. The black feather felt sharp, almost as if it was a thistle. Suddenly, before I could pull back my fingers, it was if a dark veil was pulled over my face and everything in the room seemed to stretch out and fade away. Haunting music filled my ears, and a deep, liquid voice melted inside my head. I couldn't quite hear the words, but they sounded weird – like the words Sookie had chanted in her magic act. I dropped the turban onto the floor and the light grew brighter in front of me. I stood for a minute letting my world go back to normal.

When Jasper picked up the turban and touched the feather, he said, "I think Sookie has done something terrible."

CHAPTER 17

The Nightmare Begins

JASPER HAD IT all wrong.

"Sookie would never hurt anyone!" I shouted so loud my ears rang. "Never!" And before Jasper could say another word, I tucked the stupid turban under my arm, making sure the black feather pointed away from me, and I ran out the door.

"We're supposed to stay together – it's too dark for either of us to walk home alone." Jasper stood shivering by the door as snow began to fall. "It's freezing," he complained. "That's another thing," he called after me as I raced away. "This town has never been so cold. This winter weather isn't natural."

I was a block away before I stopped, tossed the turban onto the street, and began zipping up my jacket. It was a pitch-black night, and it was bitterly cold. My fingers were so numb they fumbled with the zipper. Running from the gym was not the brightest move. But Jasper had no right to say – to imply – that my sister had .... except, maybe Sookie had done something dreadful. She might not have done it on purpose, but all the same, her new magic hobby wasn't safe. So why had Jasper gotten me so angry? I wound the wool scarf one more time around my neck and slowly picked the turban up from the ground. Snow was already sticking to the sidewalk, making it really slippery. As I made my way home, the inky night closed in, and I wished I'd waited for Jasper. It seemed tonight that I could almost hear whispers in the rush of wind. I neared my street, and Grim Hill rose before me. I could see green and yellow lights spark and flash between the snow-laden trees. It was as if some disgusting sulfurous gas had leaked out of the hill. Closing my eyes, I turned my head away.

By the time I stepped inside my house, my teeth were chattering from the cold. Sookie had already gone to bed, and Mom, who was dressed in her fuzzy white bathrobe, handed me a steaming cup of hot cocoa. As I drank it, the liquid helped me defrost while I changed into my warmest fleece pajamas and pulled on a pair of thick wool socks. I threw the turban into the black depths of my closet. I didn't want Sookie going near that creepy hat. Then I collapsed into bed and pulled up my quilt and the extra-warm wool blanket Mom gave me when the latest cold snap began.

My head spun with the worries, fears, and the grim reality that once again, there were dark mysteries happening. And I knew I had to face something. Once again, I hadn't wanted to see it. Jasper blamed Sookie, but I was the one who'd encouraged her.

Plus, what did the black feather have to do with Sookie's magic? Bit by bit, I began to recall more vividly another feather – one that made me feel quite opposite to the way the black feather made me feel. But I couldn't quite put my finger on it. Finally, I drifted into a deep, exhausted sleep.

A rattling sound seeped into my dreams. I dreamt about a chorus line of skeletons dancing on our gym stage. Click, click, click. There was a bunch of skeletons all in a row, dancing and singing, their jaw bones clickety-clacking as the sinister song spun through my ears. When a hand touched my shoulder, I sat up with a screech.

"Oh, Cat, I didn't mean to startle you," Mom soothed. "It's just that you've slept so late and you have to hurry to school."

As I stumbled out of bed, I saw that my closet door was wide open. "Were you in my closet?"

"No, Cat," said my mom. "If some of your clothes are missing I suggest you check under your bed. I haven't borrowed a single thing."

"That's not what I meant," I said a bit grouchily. I felt sweaty under my heavy pajamas, as if a fever just broke. And there was no time for a shower. Quickly I climbed into the skinny brown jeans and orange turtleneck sweater that had been rumpled up on the floor. It took that time before I could shake my nightmare off and force myself to look inside my closet. But I already knew that Sookie's purple turban wouldn't be there.

When I got downstairs, Mom handed me a peanut butter and banana sandwich. "Here, eat this in the car. Good thing I'm starting work a little later this morning so I can give you a lift to school."

"Where's Sookie?"

"Oh, she was up bright and early. She went to school with Jasper."

What was Jasper up to? He had no right bugging my sister and making her feel responsible for whatever it was that was going on in this town. If she had somehow caused Skeeter's collapse or the other kids getting sick at school, it was by accident. No doubt, there was a diabolical force behind my sister's actions. I had to find out if someone or something was pulling my sister around like a puppet. And I didn't like it one bit that she was wandering around outside with Jasper and that evil turban.

I was so rattled that I almost forgot my soccer uniform and cleats. Somehow the game today had become an after-thought. Sure I had been excited about it, but now I had to find out answers. I just couldn't miss the intramurals after school. I was team captain and my team depended on me.

Maybe there was a way I could manage to do both.

As soon as we arrived at the school, I went inside, turned around, and went out the other side of the school. I didn't care if I got in major trouble later. I was going to see if the Greystone sisters were home, and this time, I wouldn't let a few pieces of junk mail on the porch turn me away.

***

The steps and the porch of the Greystones' house had been swept clean – that was a good sign. But after I knocked and the door opened, I blurted, "Who are you?" Mom wasn't with me, but I could practically hear her shout, "Cat, how rude!"

A woman with brown hair tied in a bun, and a pencil tucked behind her ear stood in front of me. She was wearing clunky jewelry of polished stones and shells.

"I'm sorry, I mean, is Ms. Greystone home?" I tried to ask more politely.

"Which one?" she answered in a rush. "Well, no matter, as neither of them is here. They are both traveling abroad."

"Will they be back soon?"

"No, they're not planning to be back until January," she said.

I hung my head.

"Is something wrong?" she asked.

"It's just that the Greystone sisters were experts on ...

fairytales ... and I was looking for their advice."

"Who is calling?" asked the woman, and she sounded a bit odd – almost suspicious.

"Cat Peters," I said.

The woman brightened. "Cat! Alice and Lucinda told me you were a good friend of theirs. Please come in. Perhaps I can be of some help to you."

I didn't see how that could be possible, but I stepped into the front room of the Greystones' house anyway. There had been a few changes since I'd last visited in early November. Dozens of photographs set in pewter frames lined the mantle, end tables, and what they called the "credenza." In each picture, Alice and Lucinda beamed cheerfully at the camera and they had their arms wrapped tightly around each other. One photo had the Eiffel Tower in Paris in the background. The other had the Colosseum in Rome. I was pretty sure the big clock in the photograph on the end showed London's Big Ben.

"Wow," I said. "You really meant it when you said they're traveling. They didn't waste much time!"

"Mmm hmm," the woman said rather distractedly as she gathered up a huge pile of books on a blue velvet chair and offered me a seat. That was another thing that was different about the Greystones' usually tidy house. It had been overtaken by an army of books and strange artifacts of stone carvings. I even had to watch where I stepped on their Oriental carpet.

The woman finally introduced herself. "I'm Forenza Greystone. My grandfather was Lucinda and Alice's cousin. I didn't even know I had any relatives on my father's side, but they emailed me at the most perfect time and invited me to be their house sitter."

"Perfect time?" I asked, gingerly taking my seat and trying not to disturb a pile of papers perched on the arm of the chair.

"They said their home would be a very good place for me to work on my paper for the university." Forenza beamed. "I'm finishing off my doctorate in Celtic mythology and fairy lore."

Forenza started shuffling through another stack of papers on top of an oak desk. She turned to me, opened and closed her eyes several times and said, "It's my field – so perhaps I can answer any questions you have."

"Well ... do you know any legends or tales where fairies were supposed to be real creatures, and evil ... and that they enchanted people?"

Again Forenza got a look on her face that I decided was more alarmed than suspicious, but either way she wasn't smiling. I couldn't tell her the truth about everything as she'd probably phone my mother and tell her I needed to see a doctor, so I added, "You know ... for a story in my English class. Sometimes Alice Greystone helped me with my school papers."

"Ah, okay then," she smiled and looked relieved. "Well, there are lots of tales about cruel fairy enchantment making people sleep for centuries – like in Rip Van Winkle and in Sleeping Beauty." Forenza moved some of the books on the table. "And there's the story of Brigadoon where a whole town fell under an enchantment for centuries."

A whole town – my heart sped up as I thought of the children falling asleep one by one, and of the ice storms we started having, so I had to ask, "Those fairy enchantments didn't have anything to do with weird weather did they?"

Forenza shook her head, "No, I don't think so. But there

are lots of fairy legends about fairy magic influencing weather. One famous tale is about how the Oak King and the Holly King wrestle every solstice. One has to defeat the other or the seasons won't change. The Celts believed the solstice was a dangerous time for fairy meddling."

"You mean ... because maybe people could then end up having winter forever?"

Forenza gave me a long, serious look until I felt uncomfortable and had to remind her, "You know, for my story."

"I ... I don't think I know any stories like that ... Well, I'm afraid I have to be getting back to my work." She stood up, ready to escort me to the door. I had a sense that I'd upset her, but I didn't know why.

"Oh," she said. "I almost forgot that I have something for you." Forenza went to the mantel and handed me two postcards. They were postmarked from France. "These are for you – I'm sorry, I was planning to deliver them in person, but I've been so caught up in my research and all."

I said thanks and headed back to school, telling myself I'd read the postcards as I raced along so that I wouldn't be even later than I was. First, Lucinda Greystone's postcard was of a stone gargoyle that she'd sent me from a place called Notre Dame.

Dearest Cat, wrote Lucinda. You've been on my mind of late, and I just wanted to remind you: turn to the old ways of knowing.

That was disappointing. As usual, Lucinda's words were not clear. They never had been. I guess spending all that time in Fairy had made her, well, mysterious.

But when I turned over Alice Greystone's postcard of the Eiffel Tower, I came to an abrupt halt and I swear, my heart stopped.

CHAPTER 18

A Perilous Illusion

HELLO, CAT, ALICE wrote. I just wanted to drop you a quick note during our whirlwind tour. I want to make sure that the three of you are taking good care of your feathers.

Our feathers!

Of course, I'd completely forgotten that our special white feathers could help us see through fairy enchantment. Fairies have this thing called glamour where they are able to cast a spell and trick people into seeing things that aren't real, or not seeing things that are right under their noses – whatever it takes for the fairies to fool them. If there was some kind of spell floating around in this town, the feather would help me see through it. Jasper and Sookie had their feathers, too. How could I have forgotten?

I raced back to my house, burst through the door, skipped up the steps three at a time to my room, and yanked my scrap box out from under my bed. I reached inside, pulled out my feather, and hung onto it as if it was the Soccer World Cup. And I waited. And I waited some more. Last time, at Halloween, holding onto the feather made me remember things that I'd forgotten. But this time I didn't feel any different.

Maybe what I had to do was pull Jasper away from the cool kids' table at lunchtime and make him find his feather too. Together we might be able to see through any fairy enchantment to figure out what was going on. Sure of my mission, I hurried back to school.

Trying to sneak into science class late was not a great idea. I almost made it, but the classroom was so jammed with stools that I knocked one over as I tried sliding in between Mia and Amanda. Ms. Dreeble spun around from the board where she'd been writing notes.

"Caitlin Peters, why are you so late?" She peered over glasses.

"Oh. I had to pick up ... meet ..." my voice trailed off. I should have thought about an excuse. I wasn't good at making things up on the spot.

"Well, I've already sent in the attendance report. Your mother is the secretary, so I guess you'll have to explain your tardiness to her." Ms. Dreeble shook her head and went back to her lesson. "So class, can anyone give me an explanation for why we are having such dramatic weather fluctuations lately? The current weather patterns have broken all the town's records."

Our teacher knew! My heart started hammering against my ribs – Ms. Dreeble realized there was mysterious magic happening around us. Beside me, Amanda put her hand up.

"Yes, Amanda," said Ms. Dreeble.

Amanda stood up. "There is a sinister reason for our strange weather,"

Yes, yes! was shouting inside my head.

"Our town is suffering from global warming." Amanda sat down.

Huh?

"Exactly," said Ms. Dreeble.

Global warming – was that possible? And here I was telling Jasper how once you start thinking of fairies, you see them behind every problem – sour milk? It's the fairies.

Catching the flu? The fairies cast a spell. Besides, at Halloween, hadn't we managed to close the fairy portal for good? Of course this weird weather was caused by global warming, which was still worrisome, but at least everyone understood that and we could all do something to help. When the bell rang I tried to whistle cheerfully as I got ready to change classes.

Ms. Dreeble called me to her desk. "Cat, I need to rely on the team captain for the soccer intramurals. You'd better understand that it is critical that you are here on time for the bus this afternoon – at four p.m. sharp. Don't be late." Ms. Dreeble folded her arms and frowned.

"Don't worry, I'll be there." I smiled and went to history class.

But I had been so worried the evening before about what Jasper had said about Sookie that I'd forgotten about the history quiz that I was supposed to get up early and study for this morning. Clive must have been worried about Skeeter, because he didn't taunt me about my poor mark. He simply handed me back my test. He'd lost all the spark in his eyes.

"How's your brother," I whispered.

"Sleeping," said Clive. "He won't wake up, but the doctors say all his vital signs are good ... he doesn't even have a fever." Clive slumped onto his desk. "My gran wants me to go to the intramurals today anyway, but it's just not the same."

I felt bad for him – although, I didn't miss his snide remarks.

Mr. Morrows discussed the effect of steam engines on shipping and travel and how that changed the global economy in the late 1800s. Who really cared that Canada could get rubber from Brazil? When Mr. Morrows went to the board and began scribbling our history assignment for over the holiday, there was an announcement on the PA system for me to go to the office.

"It's about time the authorities caught up with you," said Mitch as he laughed.

I made sure he saw me roll my eyes at him before I left. I was worried that my mother had spotted my name missing on the attendance sheet. I dragged myself to the office as I tried to think of some excuse to tell her. The problem was I didn't want to lie, but I couldn't tell the truth. Just as I was settling into a vague excuse about having to leave school for an important errand, my mom came running out of the office and took my arm.

"Cat, I want you to hear this from me before you hear it anywhere else." Mom's voice was sharp with worry.

"What?" I asked, swallowing my heart.

"Jasper was found unconscious this morning on stage in the gym. They've taken him to the hospital."

CHAPTER 19

Magic is Secret

THIS COULDN'T BE happening!

I insisted Mom take me to see Jasper right away, but she said she'd just heard from Mia's mom who was a nurse at the hospital. The doctors didn't want the flu to spread, so Jasper wasn't allowed any visitors.

"His condition is very stable now," consoled Mom. "His vital signs are good, and that is important. You may as well go back to class, as I'm sure he's going to be all right."

Just like Skeeter, I thought.

During lunch, I sat at my table dazed while the cafeteria buzzed with noise. But it was as if a shroud of darkness had fallen over me and separated me from the rest of the students. Well, not quite, as Amarjeet sat beside me, barely touching her lunch. Mia's sandwich was still in its wrapper. When I looked over at the cool kids' table, I couldn't take my eye off the empty space where Jasper usually sat. No one had taken his seat.

"It's the fairies," I whispered. "They've hurt Jasper and the sick children."

Amarjeet said, "People get sick. There's nothing mysterious about that. My brother and Mia's sister have caught an awful flu. And now Jasper is ill. But they're going to be okay. We're still going to the intramurals."

Mia nodded wearily, as the dread that overcame me last night now spread through my body. Everyone's acceptance of the bizarre happenings was starting to feel familiar – in a totally terrible way. All those kids were practically in comas. Why weren't people freaking out? Because they don't have the feathers, I thought I heard Lucinda saying to me. They don't have glamour protection.

The afternoon dragged while I wracked my brain trying to figure out what I could do about the strange malady affecting Jasper and all of Sookie's former helpers. I had to go see Jasper for myself. But first I had to sit through the school day, pick up my sister, and then wait until Mom got home before I could go to the hospital. I wasn't going to let a "no visitors allowed" policy stop me. Waiting was torture.

When the last bell rang, I raced to Drearden elementary school and met up with Sookie as she slowly plowed through snow as deep as the tops of her blue rubber boots.

"Sookie," I called out. "Jasper is sick and in the hospital. What happened?"

"I'm freezing," Sookie complained when I caught up with her. She wiped her dripping red nose with a pink mitten. "Father Winter is taking this too far."

I was about to yell, "Didn't you just hear what I said?" but I hesitated. Come to think of it, she never even mentioned Skeeter this morning. Then, for the first time I thought carefully about what she'd been saying to me. "Just what is Father Winter carrying too far?" I asked.

"This cold weather. But it's not his fault, it's just that he's sad."

I sprung into alert mode. It was beginning to dawn on me that I should pay attention to Sookie's imaginary people. "Who is sad?"

"Father Winter," Sookie said impatiently. "I could hear his moans in the wind because he wanted to be stronger.

118

When I found the turban in the magician's trunk and put it on ..."

I noticed a suspicious bulge in Sookie's backpack that was the shape of a turban. "Go on," I said calmly, although my heart had leapt up to my throat.

Sookie glanced up at me. "When I wear the turban, he gives me magic words to help him."

Still trying to sound calm, I said, "Words like the ones you used when Skeeter disappeared?"

"Uh huh ..."

"Why didn't you tell me about those magic words," I asked.

"Magic is secret," Sookie said tersely. "It said so in the magic kit you gave me."

I studied my sister's face, but she didn't look like an evil magician, or even like someone under a spell. She barely looked nine years old.

But something was going on with her and I was sure she didn't understand. So I dug into my pocket and held up my white feather. It lit up with a purple glow, which sure made it look as if it still worked!

I handed Sookie the feather.

In Sookie's hand, the feather sparkled in every shade of blue, sapphire, indigo, and cobalt. She shrugged her shoulders. "What is it supposed to do?" she asked.

Her reaction wasn't what I'd hoped it would be. She still wasn't making connections to her actions and to what was happening to others around her. "You were with Jasper this morning, weren't you?"

Sookie looked at me. "Jasper wanted a turn in the spirit cabinet." Now she looked a bit guilty. "He asked me to make him disappear."

Of course – Jasper wouldn't have waited for me to get over my argument with him. There was an urgency we had both sensed. I choked up as I remembered he was the bravest kid I knew.

"Do you think Jasper getting sick has something to do with your magic?" I asked.

Sookie waited to answer me. Then very quietly she said, "I don't know."

There was a mystery to solve, and I was coming up with zilch. I took Sookie home and asked her to give me her turban. I yanked out the black feather and replaced it with the white one. I watched carefully as Sookie placed the turban on her head. She grew quiet, but after a minute she took the turban off.

"I don't notice much difference at all."

Why wasn't the white feather working?

Then I had an idea. As, soon as Mom got home, I raced off to the hospital determined to do whatever it took to see my friend. I just knew if I could give Jasper the feather, he would wake up and be okay.

***

More than an iron will was required to pass the nurses' desk. For the third time, I politely explained how I had to see my friend in the hospital.

"I'm sorry, young lady," the nurse said kindly, but more firmly than the way my Vice Principal, Ms. Severn, always said it. Come to think of it, they sort of looked alike – but it was more than the short gray hair. It had to do with their expressions. You totally got the impression that no excuse would ever fly past them.

As I began to despair, a person spoke behind me. "Oh, we've been waiting for this girl. Her familiar voice might help stir our son."

I turned to see Mr. and Mrs. Chung. My heart tugged as I took in their faces that were wracked with worry.

"Please, follow me, Cat," said Mr. Chung.

"I'm sorry," said the nurse, "but only immediate family is allowed into the room."

"Cat is immediate family," said Mr. Chung. The nurse flashed a look of surprise but didn't stop us.

I followed the Chungs down the hall with its green and white linoleum, and its harsh disinfectant smells stuck inside my throat. The Chungs led me into Jasper's room.

"There is a bad wind in our town," said Mr. Chung. "The elements of air and earth are not aligned. Jasper's energy flow is out of balance." We approached Jasper's hospital bed.

Jasper lay on his back – his face still, his eyes closed. He did not look at all ill. Just like all the other kids – and Buddy – he seemed healthy, except for the endless sleep. I took out my feather, and when the Chungs turned away for a moment to whisper softly to each other, I dropped it to the blanket and watched it drift to Jasper's chest. It landed.

And then in muffled cries, I tried to suppress my screams.

CHAPTER 20

Magic is Misdirection

MRS. CHUNG LEANED over the bed and stroked Jasper's forehead before giving me a puzzled look.

"She didn't see – they didn't see it!" cried a voice inside my head. "It's the glamour that's tricking their eyes!"

The room spun around me, and it was as if an eclipse covered the sun and choked out the light. But what was happening wasn't going on outside. The shock was shutting my brain down and turning my stomach inside out. I fought to stay conscious. I had to keep a hand pressed over my mouth because I couldn't stop screaming.

"What, Cat?" Mr. Chung rushed to my side, pulled me away, and sat me down on a chair beside Jasper's bed. I kept staring back at a horror.

A brown and shriveled thing with frozen, dead eyes stared up at me from the bed. Skin peeled off the gnarled, hideous creature in chunks. Instead of a mouth, a gaping hole silently screamed back at me, and a piece of gray cobweb dangled from its lips.

"This is too much for you – seeing your friend so sick," Mr. Chung said in alarm. "I didn't mean to unsettle you."

I couldn't bear to be in the room one second longer, but I had to fight with myself not to terrify the Chungs any more than I had. I also had to get that feather back – maybe my friend's life counted on it. "I ... I'm late, I've got to go ..." I managed to say, but when I reached out toward that nightmare in the bed to grab my feather, I gagged.

"Are you going to get sick?" Mr. Chung asked, sounding panicked. "I should get the doctor." But I shook my head and stumbled out of the room.

"Cat, what are you doing here?" I heard Mia's mother call after me. I started running.

My friend? That wasn't my friend, that ... it ... wasn't even human. I clutched the feather and raced out of the hospital. Once outside, I chugged in the sharp, brutally cold air and let out a piercing scream. It wasn't until I'd run all the way home, slipping and sliding in the snow and ice, and stood panting on my front porch that I managed to get my brain working again. I looked for Sookie and found her in her room. She was sitting on her bed, covering her ears.

"What's wrong?" I asked.

"Father Winter is laughing," she said in a voice that managed to sound annoyed and frightened at the same time.

Carefully, I listened to the shrill wind as it blew against the window. Perhaps it did sound like a menacing chuckle. Taking my feather, I went over to Buddy's cage. I poked the feather through the bars and began tickling the hibernating hamster.

"What are you doing?" Sookie rushed to my side.

"Stay away," I said, not wanting to frighten her. "Our feathers still work," I said. "There is enchantment going on, and someone has been deceiving our eyes. This isn't really Buddy."

But of course, telling Sookie this only made her more determined to see what was going on.

"That's not Buddy," said Sookie in surprise. "It's a piece of wood."

She was right. The chunk of wood was roughly hewed

into the shape of a hamster with a round body and tiny face. I forced myself to picture the thing I saw lying in the hospital bed, and I shuddered. I realized it had been a stump of wood with crudely carved human features. The peeling skin had been chiseled bark that revealed lumpy chunks of raw wood – a horrible Pinocchio face, but not Jasper at all. Except to everyone else who didn't have the feather – who fell for the fairy glamour – it was Jasper. His mom and dad thought the stump of wood in the hospital bed was him, just as Sookie and I thought this piece of branch had been Buddy.

"Magic is misdirection," Sookie said quietly as she held my white feather and stared down at the piece of wood in her hamster cage. "You think one thing is happening, but something else is going on instead. I thought I was doing magic tricks, but it was Father Winter tricking me. He stole Buddy. That's despicable."

"Sookie, someone is stealing all the children, not just Buddy. It happens when you make them disappear. Do you understand the words to your magic incantations?"

"No. And I only can say them when I wear the turban. You might not like it, but we're going to need it." Sookie got off her bed. I followed her downstairs where Mom was rattling around in the kitchen.

"Cat?" said Mom in surprise. "Why aren't you on the school bus heading for the intramurals?"

Slamming to a halt as if I'd just banged into a wall, the cold realization hit me. I'd completely forgotten! I was winded. But no matter how much I wanted to go to the intramurals, I couldn't leave anyway. Not with the wicked events surrounding me – events I was only beginning to understand. I had to save my friend and find all the real children – not the pieces of wood taking their places.

"Cat ... why didn't you go?" Mom asked me again, her voice tinged with worry.

"Jasper," was all I could say.

"Mrs. Chung called me. She said she was worried you might be getting sick too."

Right away Mom was feeling my forehead. "You do look pale."

"I'm fine," I said.

"Sorry you missed the game," Mom said quietly, before she went back to cooking dinner. "Just to be on the safe side, I think you should go to bed early tonight and get some rest. I don't want you to come down with whatever it is that's going around."

Sookie and I went to the den to escape Mom's worried glances. I kept a very close eye on Sookie as she slipped on the turban, which now had the black feather attached to it.

"Now do you remember the words you say with your magic?" I asked.

Sookie nodded, but before she said them out loud, I signaled for her to stay silent. Handing her a sheet of paper, I said, "It's probably safer if you write them down."

Grabbing a purple crayon, Sookie hesitated. "They're kind of hard to spell." She closed her eyes and said, "Oh. If I pretend Teacher is writing them on the board ..." and then she began to scribble.

The words weren't English, and they did look hard to spell. But I'd seen those types of words before – ones that were written so differently from the way they sounded. Samhain came to mind – a word that was actually pronounced Sow-en. That was a word the ancient Celts used.

The Celts!

I pulled out Lucinda Greystone's gargoyle postcard, which had "Turn to the old ways of knowing" written on it. A dim lightbulb lit up inside my head. Maybe ... just maybe I knew where we might find a little help.

***

There was something peculiar about the Greystone sisters' yard. While the outermost edges of the grass had as much snow as every other home on the street, by the time I reached the end of the sidewalk, there was only a dusting of frost on their steps. When I looked up, out of all the white roofs that stretched out for blocks, the Greystones' roof remained black without one bit of snow on it. Winter was being kept at a distance. Crazy.

I could tell by the light behind the window shade that Forenza was home. But after I'd slammed the door knocker five times, there was still no answer. So I took off my gloves and pounded on the door.

Finally it opened a crack, and I could see inside. Forenza was wearing gardening gloves, and she had garden sheers in one hand. Pine needles were caught in her hair, and sprigs of mistletoe were tied around her neck in a huge green and white necklace.

"Hello again," she smiled in a nervous way. "Sorry, I was absorbed in a podcast on ancient languages, and I didn't hear you knock."

Forenza opened the door wider and invited me inside. Wow. She was really into the season. Since we'd talked this morning, she'd decorated the house. Boughs of evergreen jammed so tightly in vases almost toppled from the mantel, coffee table, and end tables. Lit candles were set on every available surface casting shadows that flickered eerily around the house. About a dozen holly wreaths hung from the walls, and streamers of ivy dangled from the ceiling.

Sookie and I had been so caught up in soccer matches and the talent contest, we hadn't even talked about hauling out our boxes of decorations from the attic.

There wasn't much time, so I had to get down to business. I'd sneaked out of the house as I knew Mom would freak out if I was wandering around all pale in the cold. Even though I felt okay, I was worried big time, but Sookie said she'd cover for me until dinner.

"I was wondering if you maybe recognize these words," I asked, defrosting in the warm glow of the Greystones' parlor. Logs burned in the fireplace, filling the room with the scent of wood smoke. I usually loved the smells of Christmas, but tonight I didn't feel excited at all. Instead my hand trembled and my stomach turned as I handed Forenza the sheet of Sookie's purple crayoning.

"Bear leat, means to take away," said Forenza. But when she pronounced those words it was "bow- la." And here I was thinking Sookie had been mispronouncing "voila."

Fuadaigh an leanbh," Forenza said. "Tabhair dom an mhaide." Only when she pronounced them, the words came out, "foothee-on-lanive", and "Thoe-rum-on wa-ju," just like Sookie's magical incantation.

"Those are all Celtic words," said Forenza. Her eyes widened. "'Take the child, bring the wood.' That sounds like a changeling story," she said with a visible shudder.

"What's a changeling," I asked, thinking that this didn't sound good ... not good at all.

"Only one of the darkest legends in fairy lore," Forenza

said and she handed me back the paper as if she couldn't get rid of it fast enough.

The color drained from her face.

CHAPTER 21

The Darkest Day

"**DO YOU BELIEVE** in coincidences, Cat?" Forenza asked in a voice that I swear sounded petrified.

"Not always." There, I'd said it out loud to an adult. Too many things were connected in this town. And I was beginning to wonder if Forenza sensed that.

"Well, it is sort of odd," Forenza tried to laugh but didn't quite succeed. "Here you show up on my porch asking a question about dark fairy lore, when right now it is December twentieth. Today is the winter solstice, the day with the least amount of sunlight, so we're heading into the longest night of the year.

"Do you remember I'd mentioned the Celts believed the winter solstice was a time of danger?" she asked. "How they worried if winter would ever leave?" Forenza pointed out the vases of greenery. "During this night, trays of bread were left on tables, and boughs of evergreen and branches of holly were brought in to offer people protection from the malevolence of fairy folk. They were worried about whether the Holly King would allow spring to return to their village."

The Celts understood the haunts of fairies. I'd turned to their legends and myths before, during Halloween. At that time the fairies had been up to no good and had tried casting spells on us humans to keep the doorway between our worlds open and to allow them through. The Celts had certain practices to keep fairies away, and they knew when it was a dangerous time – when the door between our worlds opened and put us in peril.

I gulped, not wanting to think about that again because I thought we were supposed to have been safe. But now I needed to hear about what the Celts believed. "What has the winter solstice to do with – what did you call them? – changelings?" I asked in the flickering candle light.

"Those words you showed me are incantations that would invite a fairy to do a swap," said Forenza. "The fairies would steal away a child."

"Why would they do that?" I asked in kind of a strangled way.

"Fairies desire human children, especially this time of year," said Forenza in a hushed voice. And then she did something strange – well, even stranger. Forenza walked to the mantel and picked up a small silver bell. She gave it a ring. "More fairy protection." She smiled apologetically. "Not that I'm superstitious – this is more of a ... a ... Christmas tradition. As I was explaining, some legends say fairies use children for slaves, or sometimes keep children as pets. But other legends hint to a darker purpose ..." Forenza rang the bell again and its jingle chimed as she walked over to a glass lamp and lit a flame. "I think we should have a little more light for such a spooky tale, don't you?"

I nodded even though it was as bright as day inside that house. Forenza had every single lamp on. "You mentioned fairies had a darker purpose ... for stealing young children?" I asked.

"For mortal blood," Forenza said in a strained voice. "Children's blood is powerful, so fairies might use it during the solstice, in order to keep the door between our worlds open. By using fairy changelings and exchanging the children for fairy wood enchanted to look like the person it replaces, no one knows the children are missing, and no one suspects what the fairies are up to, so no one tries to stop them."

"What would the fairies do with the doorway open?"

"Appease the Holly King and keep winter going forever in the village," she explained. "But that's just a story made up by an ancient superstitious people."

I didn't think Forenza believed that it was just a story – her eyes darted around the room as if she was expecting to see a ghost ... or an evil fairy. There was something about the Holly King that kept turning over in my mind.

"When you talked earlier about the battle between the two fairies – the Oak King and the Holly King – did the Celts ever call these fairies by other names – were there any other legends tied to them?"

"Oh, certainly," said Forenza, and she finally put down the bell and picked up a book on the table. She flipped through its pages. "The Holly King has several names: the green man, the green fairy ..." she said as she began ushering me out the door.

"You should hurry home, Cat. This is a good night for battening down the hatches. Really, you must hurry," she urged. Grabbing several sprigs of holly from a vase, she tucked them into my jacket pocket. Then she looked at me for a moment and asked me to wait.

"Take this." Forenza handed me a small branch with round red berries. "Rowan is excellent fairy protection, not that fairies are ..." but she didn't bother saying fairies weren't "real."

As I made my way down the stairs, Forenza called to me one last time.

"I just remembered. Another name for the Holly King is

Father Winter."

Oh Sookie, I thought as a chill wrapped around my heart. What have you done?

As soon as I left Forenza's snow-free yard and headed out for my own house, I noticed there was something horribly wrong.

CHAPTER 22

The Longest Night

I MADE MY way home from Forenza's while a blizzard now raged and snow and sleet flew in my face. The wind screeched, and the sun began to sink in the sky. I spotted Mr. Keating standing outside his store, knee-deep in the snow. He wasn't wearing a hat or a coat, and his apron flapped in the wind. Snow kept falling on him, covering him until he began to look like a snowman.

"Mr. Keating, aren't you cold?" I asked, surprised that he wasn't trying to haul in his barrels of apples or potatoes before they froze.

He turned to me in an unsteady, half-frozen way, but he smiled when he said, "Oh, hi there, Cat."

"Shouldn't you be getting inside?" I asked again. "It's freezing out here."

When Mr. Keating didn't move, I tugged his apron and led him inside his shop. "I think maybe you better stay here," I said. When I closed the shop door and the bell jingled, Mr. Keating finally mumbled "Thanks," and I left the shop. As I looked back, the snow piled up on the barrels outside the store and began covering the Emporium's windows. Then the shop's awning buckled and heaps of snow blocked the door. At least Mr. Keating was now safe inside. I began plowing my way through the snow again.

The streets were deserted and I had no idea why. Why weren't people rushing to get home and out of the bad weather? When I turned down Mia's street, a few blocks away from my house, a car was stuck in the middle of the road. The windshield was covered in snow, except for one little spot. When I looked inside, I saw Mia's mother sitting there. I knocked on the car door.

For a while Mia's mother didn't notice me, but I kept knocking louder and louder. Finally, she rolled down the window and didn't even react to the pile of snow that landed in her lap.

"Aren't you going inside?" I asked. "Isn't it cold in the car?" Like Mr. Keating, Mia's mom wasn't wearing a coat – she only had on a sweater buttoned up over her nurse's uniform. First, she blinked at me as if she didn't hear me, then she slowly shook her head.

"Cat? What are you doing here?" She sounded groggy – as if she'd just woken up from a dream. "I ... just dropped ... Mia off ... to catch the bus for the soccer game. Why ... why aren't you on the bus?"

I wanted to say, "Because soccer is the last thing on my mind, and I completely forgot about the game today." But I didn't say that. I was worried about Mia's mother. The bus left a couple of hours ago, so she must have been sitting here in her car for a while. "You'd better let me help you," I told her.

Just like with Mr. Keating, I had to lead her to her house, take the keys from her hand, unlock the door, and help her inside. An urgent voice in my head said, "Get home, Cat, something is very wrong here, and you'd better check on your own family." After closing the door to Mia's house, I took off.

My feet skidded on some ice and I fell. Something was happening here that was so wicked. How did I ever think for a moment that it could have been due to climate change? Sure, lots of places got blizzards in December, but not in this town; the locals said we got snow only in January. Before we moved here, we'd lived a lot farther north and hadn't seen weather like this in that town. Besides, it wasn't simply the snow – it was the weird way the temperature fluctuated from day to day. The weather had become unpredictable right after that first ice storm on Sookie's birthday ... except that one weekend before the soccer match. Wait a minute – that was also the weekend Buddy first got sick and Sookie was too devastated to practice her magic. Of course! Whenever Sookie practiced her magic show, cold blasted through our town. How did I miss that connection – that when Sookie made things disappear, the temperature plunged? I sat up rubbing my arm. Lately, Sookie had been practicing a lot of magic, I thought as I looked around.

Snow piled high on everyone's roofs and dripped down. It was as if a baker had gone crazy icing gingerbread houses. Treacherous icicles hung from all the telephone wires, and in a few place I could see the lines were down. The sidewalks weren't shoveled, nor were the streets cleared of snow. Frigid blue clouds hovered, shaking down endless snow at us. Our town looked like a tiny village trapped inside a snow globe.

It was even more than that, though. Today was the winter solstice and there was a different kind of chill in the air, as if something evil was creeping into the streets. I reached into my pocket and clasped my white feather. Pulling myself up from the sidewalk, I stumbled in the direction of my house. As I walked, flashing Christmas lights seemed to wink at me in a cruel way, letting me know that they were in on a terrible secret. Trouble is coming, wink-wink, right, Cat? Even the Christmas wreaths that dangled from doors suddenly looked to me like hangmen's nooses, waiting to choke any unsuspecting victim who came too close. When I turned the corner and headed down my block, I swear the black coal eyes of a snowman followed me. What was happening?

Then, as I looked up toward Grim Hill looming above my street, I could see a turquoise fog of enchantment spilling down and rolling over our town. I stared in horror as the blue-green fog reached out from the hill and stretched like arms until it surrounded us and disappeared into the darkening horizon.

Could others see this? It occurred to me that if this was the case, then I wouldn't have to fight the fairies alone; I could get help. I broke into a run. Sure, I wasn't running at lightning speed in the snow and ice, but I moved a lot faster. Once up my steps, I burst through the door.

"Mom! Mom!" I shouted. "We've got to get help. We've got some kids to rescue. We also need to call the fire department or the police. Something bad is happening to our friends and neighbors, and we've got to figure out a way to get people out of this town – fast." I collapsed on the overstuffed chair, gasping for breath, and only then did I begin to notice that it wasn't much warmer inside our house than out in the snow. I wasn't even breaking a mild sweat even though I had on a wool hat, thick gloves, a scarf, and a heavy coat. The snow on my boots hadn't even begun to melt.

"Mom?" I called as anxiousness crept into my voice. I went into the kitchen, ready to call her again, but the word caught in my throat. Any hope I had of getting help slid away. Tears would have stung my eyes, but it was too cold for tears.

My mother sat stiffly in her kitchen chair. The back door was open and snow drifted in, settling in heaps on the floor and dusting the oak table. A thin sheet of ice coated the coffee in my mother's yellow mug, and her fingers locked around its handle. First I shoved the door shut, cutting off the wind and snow. Then I ran to the couch and grabbed the afghan and covered my mother with it.

"Please," I cried. "Mom, please say something." I lifted her fingers from her coffee cup and began rubbing her hand and arm.

Mom looked at me; she wasn't frozen, or even unconscious. But she wasn't herself, either. Slowly she blinked her eyes as she stared at me, and her words came out as cold and as stiff as she looked.

"Almost didn't make it back in ... phone lines are down... and there's been an avalanche on the edge of town. No one is getting through ... and ... the school bus with the soccer team is turning back ... they are stuck in the snow ... but they should be back soon ... Looks like you didn't miss the game after all ... Cat."

"Why would you say that, Mom? Who cares about soccer, you must see what's going on now, right? You must know something really bad is happening here with all the sick kids and the blizzard. Look at Grim Hill, can you see ..."

My words died on my lips. Mom was staring out the window all right – she was staring up at Grim Hill. But I realized she wasn't seeing anything, or at least anything I would understand. It felt as if my stomach was going to heave up everything I'd eaten during the day. I watched my mother's indigo eyes fade until I was looking into two pools of pale ice.

"Where's Sookie?" I asked suddenly. "Mom, where's Sookie?" Then I spotted the small boot prints denting the snow on the floor and leading to the door.

"Where did Sookie go?" I asked in even more alarm.

My mother kept looking out the window and up at Grim Hill. "Sookie said she had to go find Jasper and Skeeter ... she couldn't wait for you any longer ..."

"What do you mean?" My heart lurched in shock. "You just let her walk out into this weather? Mom ..."

But my mother didn't say another word; she only stared out the window.

CHAPTER 23

Vanishing Act

OF COURSE I had to chase after Sookie, but the red kitchen clock ticking away distracted me. Forenza had said the winter solstice was a perilous time for humans, when fairies from the otherworld could break through to our world and wreak havoc. But the clock hands kept ticking, as if they intended to race through the darkest day of the year and not give me any time to stop the fairies.

Something was happening to the grown-ups around me; it was as if the cold and ice had wrapped around their minds and hearts. No one noticed what was going on, and worse, no one seemed able to care. The first thing I had to do was get my sister, and maybe having that one clear plan would keep me from freaking out.

I ran upstairs and got the quilt from my bed and then went back down and wrapped it around Mom. Then I opened my backpack that contained the rowan branch Forenza had given me – the branch she said had power over fairies. Its red berries stained the inside of my pack in what looked like blood. What else had she said would give someone fairy protection? Oh yeah, I took my mother's china dinner bell and some slices of bread from the cupboard.

Grabbing the flashlight and the garden shears from the kitchen closet, I said bye to my mom and told her I'd be back soon. Then I shut the back door as if I was just going off to school or to visit a friend, except my mother didn't answer.

Instead, she sat frozen in her chair. I ran down the porch steps and headed toward the last place on Earth I ever wanted to go – Grim Hill.

The path I used to climb every day in October was a lot narrower now. The trees had grown in closer, hugging the edges of the path, their huge evergreen branches reaching out as if to grab me. The light from my flashlight bobbed along the path and out past the trees. I almost expected a wolf to come waltzing out looking for Red Riding Hood, or if I went off the path into the woods, I thought I might stumble across a gingerbread house with an evil witch inside. I shoved those thoughts out of my mind, kept my head down, and focused my flashlight on Sookie's footprints.

As I climbed the hill, the snowflakes became larger until first they were as big as my fist, and then they grew almost as large as the doilies on Alice Greystone's coffee table. The air was thickly scented with cedar and pine. Except, instead of being invigorating, it was as if the smells clogged my brain, and a voice kept whispering, "Don't worry, Cat – it's all fine. Just have fun, make snowballs, and play in the snow." I took my gloves off, clasped my white feather with one hand and loosened my scarf to let the bitter air help me keep my focus.

When I reached the top of the hill, what had once been Grimoire School was nothing but rubble. Brambles already covered a lot of the decayed stone. This is where Sookie's footprints disappeared. She must have climbed onto the rocks and made her way to the middle of the brick and stone.

I couldn't see traces of Sookie's footprints anywhere else, but I knew where she went. Forced to admit the enchantment of Fairy had never quite left Sookie after

Halloween, I knew she could still hear sounds and haunting music coming from that hill – sounds that no one else heard. I bet she had no trouble finding her way back into Fairy. I thought I'd just be able to follow her path, but I should have realized getting into Fairy would require a little bit of magic, or at least a connection that I didn't have.

"Sookie, what have you done?" I muttered, sick with worry. But the big question was, What was I going to do?

I slumped down onto what had once been part of Grimoire's wall, but currently the rocks looked like a flattened grave stone. As I sat in the cold dark, I heard a faint chirp. Next to me on the stone sat a bird – a robin. It was shivering and I could see its little red chest puffing in and out.

"Oh, poor thing," I said. "What are you doing here in the middle of winter? Why didn't you fly south with the other birds?" I reached into my pack and took out the bread I had brought with me for fairy protection. I had never figured out exactly how I was supposed to use it anyway – what, throw a slice of whole wheat at a fairy? Instead I tore the bread up into tiny pieces and fed it to the robin. He gobbled greedily and flew into my hands to eat the last crumbs. Briefly I covered him to warm him up, and when I opened my hands he flew up on my shoulder. When I turned my head we gazed eye to eye. Then the robin flew into the branches, and he sang as he flew. His song gave me a new surge of energy. When I got up from the stone, it was as if my head cleared.

There was another way into Grim Hill and the fairy world. There was also a group of people who might be able to help me. I needed to get to the high school where the spirit cabinet sat on the gym stage – it had to be a link to the fairy world. If my mother had been right about the bus turning back from the game, then it would be arriving at the school any minute.

I had a feeling there would be kids on that bus who could help me – kids who hadn't fallen under the mysterious winter spell ... yet.

CHAPTER 24

Entombed in Ice

I HAD TO hurry to meet the school bus before all the kids on it scattered. With a burst of energy, I jumped off the stone and left the rubble of Grimoire School behind. Then I set out toward the other side of Grim Hill. That side led back to the center of town and close to the high school. Using my backpack as a make-shift toboggan, I slipped and slid all the way down the hill, hitting low branches as snow fell on my head and left an icy trail down my neck and back.

At the bottom of the hill the snow stopped falling. But as I walked toward the high school another icy blast put everything in a deep freeze. Ice was now coating my eyelashes and any hair not tucked in my hat grew stiff. I worried that those strands might snap. My frozen breath floated behind me like a ghost.

In the sky, a few purple clouds parted, allowing the waning moon – white as a slice of bone – to come out and cast shadows over the main street of town. Silence hung like a blanket muffling any sound, even the whispery swish of my boots as I half-skated on the frozen snow. Twice I stopped to lead adults into their shops if they were unfortunate enough not to get inside before the enchantment took over. Like Mr. Keating, they stood frozen in the eerie grey light, but they would follow me if I led them inside. Then, like Mom, they shut down and their eyes stared blankly out toward the snow-covered streets.

I now realized Forenza understood quite a lot about fairy enchantment, even if it terrified her so much that she refused to admit that she believed. She hadn't been telling me simple fairytales. She'd been warning me that if I didn't stop the fairy enchantment before the end of the solstice tonight, our town would be locked in an icy prison and would be frozen in time. I bet no one on the outside would even notice us slipping away from this world. Now it wasn't only about finding Sookie or rescuing Jasper and the other children. I thought back to my dream of dancing skeletons – these fairies were turning our town into an icy tomb. I had to stop this winter spell.

What other Celtic tradition had I seen Forenza use to protect herself during the solstice? I tried remembering ... Celts had used bells and lanterns and burning Yule logs to keep them safe. One thing I'd learned at Halloween was that Celts were proactive against fairies, so I trusted they knew how to protect themselves on the longest night of the year. Light seemed important, and I would make sure I used a lot of light.

As I got closer to the schoolyard I could see the school bus. It looked as if it had spun out and fishtailed in the snow. The side of the bus had hit the school gate, toppling down the chain-link fencing and cutting off the exit from the bus. Even though my lungs burned and my side ached, I began to run.

When I reached the bus, the emergency door crashed open. Kids began to wrestle themselves out of the tilting bus and land on the snow outside.

"Wait!" I heard Clive call from inside the bus. "There's something wrong with the bus driver and the teachers – they aren't moving."

Or they're beginning to freeze, I thought. One thing I'd

come to understand about fairy enchantment is that adults succumbed to spells first, never quite realizing the otherworld sometimes overlapped ours. Children noticed boogey men, invisible friends, fairies, and magic until adults convinced them otherwise. I wondered if I would be able to make my friends realize what was happening – we weren't quite adults, but we weren't children either. Watching how slowly some of the kids were moving around outside, I figured it could go either way at age thirteen. Tossing my pack on the ground, I climbed onto the school bus.

"You're a little late for the soccer game ..." said Clive, but his words drifted into a whisper. He rubbed his eyes and looked at all the snow outside, and then back at the teachers. "What's going on?" he asked, and this time he didn't even try to sound remotely sarcastic.

I waved my white feather in front of Amarjeet and Mia. "Remember what happened at Halloween," I said. Amarjeet stroked the feather with her fingers, and her eyes widened in surprise as she looked at the ice-covered town and at our teachers frozen in their seats. Then Mia touched the feather, looked around, and gasped.

"What?" asked Clive.

"Fairy magic," whispered Mia.

"Don't you mean Santa and his elves?" said Clive, now sounding more like himself. "C'mon, we've got to get an ambulance for Mr. Morrows and Ms. Dreeble."

"No ambulance will come," I said. "But I think the teachers will be okay – well, okay as any other adult in town tonight. But we'd better get everyone inside the school where it'll be warm," I said, reaching out for Ms. Dreeble's arm. It was Clive's turn to look surprised as I led Ms. Dreeble from her seat. Mia and Amarjeet followed my lead and helped the bus driver and Mr. Morrows from their seats. They meekly followed us out of the bus, and Ms. Dreeble didn't object when I fished through her pocket and found the keys for the school.

We brought the adults inside and sat them in the front office. Already most of the kids from the bus had slowed down and began sitting in the hallway. It was getting colder in the school as the furnace tried to keep up with the frigid temperature outside. Zach and I grabbed emergency blankets out of the storage closet and began covering everyone. I started passing my white feather around to the few of us who were still moving.

"Hey," I said to Mitch and Emily. "Grab the flashlights from the utility cupboards and pass them out to Clive, Mia, Amarjeet, and Zach. Tell them to meet us in the gym.

When the others arrived, I'd been standing rooted to the gym floor, staring up at the spirit cabinet on the stage.

"So what's the plan, are we ... " Mia's voice faded as she caught sight of the cabinet.

No one needed a magic feather to see the light pouring out from behind the cabinet's star and moon curtain, and wrapping itself around the trunk. The other kids gathered at the bottom of the stage and stared in bewilderment at the glowing cabinet.

I gulped and said, "Guess I'm going inside that trunk. I need one of you to chant these words once I'm inside." Reaching in my pack, I grabbed the Celtic incantation that Sookie had written in purple crayon, the words Forenza had translated for me, and I handed it to Amarjeet.

Amarjeet held the paper in her hand, looked down at it, and then up at the mysterious light flowing from the spirit cabinet. "My brother went into that trunk, and when he came out I thought he got sick. But something else happened to him, didn't it, Cat?

"The fairies got him," I said quietly. "They bewitched a piece of wood so that we thought it was Raj, but it wasn't. He's really in Fairy."

Mia let out a moan. "And my sister?"

"In Fairy," I said. "So are Jasper and all the other kids who were Sookie's apprentices." Then I looked at Clive. "Skeeter, too – the fairies took your brother and left a fairy changeling in his place."

Clive stared at me in disbelief.

"Huh? Changeling? What about your sister?" asked Emily.

"She's also in Fairy now." I didn't bother mentioning that Sookie went there by choice. "We've got to get them all back. I think when we do, we can also stop what's happening to the town. We can break the spell and end this deep freeze."

Before anyone could say anything, I pulled back the curtain. I shielded my eyes against the blinding blue light. "Once I'm inside, read the words on the page, and make sure you pronounce them the way they were translated," I said.

"Wait." Amarjeet had put her hand on my shoulder. "If you disappear, then we lose the only one who knows how to fight the fairies."

I didn't feel like much of an expert. "But I have a plan," I said. "Once I'm on the Fairy side of Grim Hill, I'll ring the bell I've brought with me. Celts used bells, and I think it's because their sound can break through fairy enchantment. I bet fairies don't like the ringing. You should then be able to climb the hill and follow the sound of the bell. The ringing should lead you to a door buried under the rubble of Grimoire School." This was the door I had discovered just before the Halloween match and I'd hoped I would never have to pass through it again. "Once you open it, there will be a passageway leading into Grim Hill and out to the Fairy side."

"Let me do it," said Amarjeet. "I'll take the bell, and I guarantee you, I won't stop ringing it until you come and find me."

"But ..." was all I could say.

"Amarjeet's right," said Mia. "It should be one of us."

I had forgotten that my friends had been brave when we battled the fairies before. "Okay, maybe ..."

"It should be me," Amarjeet insisted. "My brother's been gone the longest, and I'm so worried – I need to see him."

I handed Amarjeet the bell. "Remember ..." I began.

"No kidding," she said, and she began ringing the bell as soon as she stepped inside the trunk.

CHAPTER 25

Celtic Magic

MITCH, EMILY, MIA, Zach, and Clive watched as I chanted the first part of the incantation, the part about taking away the child.

"Fuadaigh an leanbh," I said. I waited a moment and tore open the curtain.

Amarjeet had disappeared.

Everyone gasped and Mia let a small cry escape. Even though they had seen Sookie do the same thing on the night of the talent contest, we understood now it wasn't an illusion. This was black magic – something supernatural – just as Jasper had said. And Amarjeet was in Fairy now.

"Okay, we have to move fast." I headed for the gym door.

"Wait a minute."

Clive stood on the stage. His arms were crossed and he had a scowl on his face. "How did you make Amarjeet disappear? I never figured out how your sister managed to make Skeeter disappear either."

Okay, almost everyone had it figured out. There wasn't time to explain, so I said, "If you want to help us get your brother home, then follow us up Grim Hill."

"My brother is sick in the hospital ... he ..." Clive seemed confused. He looked outside as Mitch opened the door. Snow blew in. Clive stared at the snow, and then he looked back at the cabinet. "Except ... there is something creepy going on,

149

isn't there? That light shining out of the cabinet ... and the weather and our teachers ... this isn't ... normal ..."

Clive had run out of smart remarks as I led Mia, Zach, Emily, and Mitch out the gym door and into the freezing wind. Then he shouted, "Wait!" and ran to catch up with us.

The streets were deserted, and all the cars, fences, and signposts were buried in white as if a volcano had erupted in a fountain of snow, covering everything in its path. Sound froze, too. For a while, we didn't hear anything as we walked along the empty streets. But as we began climbing Grim Hill, first we heard the snapping of twigs, then the moaning of the wind, and I began to wonder if I heard baleful mutterings. Then we heard howling ahead of us on the path and a horrible shriek, so we huddled closer together and moved faster. No one turned back.

When we got near the top of the hill, I began to move even faster because I began to hear a faint chime. "C'mon!" I shouted. "I hear Amarjeet's bell."

We followed the chiming to the rubble of what was left of Grimoire school until the bell grew louder and there was a definite clanging underneath the rock and brick. Mitch and Zach cleared away the bigger stones, and we saw the door and yanked it open. A stone staircase led below the ground, and I recognized that staircase as the one I had discovered in Grimoire's library. Those steps led to Fairy.

"Hurry," said Mia. "I've got to get my sister out of there." She stepped down to the first stair.

Emily hesitated, then she said with a gulp, "I'll go too ... I ... I'm losing a lot of money since those kids I babysit got sick." Then she tried to smile, but I knew she was scared. That made me think she was even more courageous.

"Wait," I said. "We'll need guards at the door to

make sure the kids get out and that the fairies stay inside. Emily, Zach, and Mitch, I think you should stay behind and make sure no one gets through that door except humans." The fairies weren't going to just stand by and let us rescue our brothers and sisters and then shut the door between our worlds.

Again I thought about Forenza and how she'd made sure the Greystone sisters' house remained free of the fairy spell. I closed my eyes and pictured the Christmas trimmings she'd decorated around the rooms.

"We're going to need lots of evergreen and light," I said. "The Celts burned a Yule log all night during the solstice and threw holly and ivy into the fire to keep them safe from dark magic." Then as my ideas flowed, I said to everyone, "If we can keep a fire going at the entrance of the staircase, maybe the smoke and light from our fire will keep the fairies out of our world until the solstice passes."

Digging the garden shears from my backpack, I handed them to Emily. "We're going to need branches of holly and ivy – go." Then I turned to Zach and said, "You stay behind with Emily. Find a log, look under the rocks, and try to find a dry one for a Yule fire – hurry." Zach and Emily raced to the edges of the rubble and began gathering greenery for the fire.

I turned to Mitch, "Just a hunch, but I'm guessing you know how to keep a fire going." It wasn't really a hunch. Mitch got in big trouble once in science for using the Bunsen burner to smolder a bunch of his notes.

Mitch produced his own matches.

"Remember – don't let the fire go out," I told him.

"Who made you boss?" Clive turned toward the steps. "I'm going down to see what's there."

"But how will we get the kids?" Mia asked me,

ignoring Clive.

"I'm hoping we'll figure that out when we find Amarjeet," I said. Emily had come back with an armful of holly, and I handed a branch of it to Mia and to Clive for protection. "This might help."

Everyone was willing to take on the fairies – however, I thought Clive was only coming along out of curiosity. He had no real sense of the danger.

"Keep your heads down," I said as Mia and Clive followed me into the underground passageway.

I couldn't help but feel sorry for Clive and Mia. They had no idea what they were getting themselves into.

Whatever it was, it wouldn't be good.

CHAPTER 26

A Human Sacrifice

WE CREPT DOWN the stone stairway in the dark.

"We don't exactly want to announce our arrival," I said, "so we'd better keep our flashlights off."

There were scurrying sounds on the staircase and a whooshing noise from above, but if it bothered Clive and Mia, they didn't say anything. The chiming of the bell became louder and a sphere of red light grew at the bottom of the staircase until we stepped outside under a sky of red and orange clouds that glowed like molten lava.

"What ... where ..." Clive stood outside the tunnel and stared at the pitch-black trees with huge, silver leaves. Even though there was lots of snow on the ground, flowers with fleshy purple petals and dangerous black thorns clustered next to the trees. "Flowers, leaves, and snow all at once – it's as if all the seasons collided together right on this spot." He shook his head.

Day and night collided as well – while the sky was fiery bright, it cast a twilight glow, and long black shadows stretched out over the snowy landscape.

"Was it like this before in Fairy?" Mia asked me breathlessly. "Were the sun, moon, and stars all out at the same time?"

I looked up at the red sky and stared at stars that were a lot bigger than any stars I'd ever seen. They were as pointy as crystal Christmas tree ornaments. Shaking my head, I said, "Last time it looked more like fall, except ... different ..." There were things in Fairy you just couldn't explain.

"This place gives me the creeps," Clive said quietly. "It's spooky, like some kind of alien planet."

Or maybe it could be explained – Clive did have a point.

"So ... okay ... I am definitely in some strange land ... so if there were such things as fairies ... what would they look like?" Clive asked in a way that made me think this weirdness was finally sinking in for him. "Can't we just grab them by their little wings and tell them to leave our town alone?" Now he was trying to sound cocky, but he couldn't quite pull it off this time.

"The Grimoire girls ... fairies ... look like us," said Mia. Her face grew so pale, freckles almost leaped off her face. "... like us, only ..." Mia pointed to a thorny flower, "See how that rose is different from any flower you've ever seen? The same is true with fairies. They're more ..."

"More what?" asked Clive.

"More ... beautiful and more terrifying ..."

The way Mia said that gave me the chills and it silenced Clive right away. Then the peal of a bell rang nearby, and we followed the sound through a break in the trees. We stepped out into a tiny clearing, and my heart sped up.

Amarjeet, with her arm around Raj, stood with Sookie in the middle of the clearing. Mia's little sister and all Sookie's magician's assistants crowded behind them. Amarjeet was shaking the bell, and its rings sent echoes around the circle of black and silver trees.

I drew in a sharp breath as Mia and Clive choked back a muffled cry when we spotted shadows spilling from the trees – that is, what looked like shadows until they came closer. Then those shadows began turning into black-haired, green-eyed Grimoire girls with their treacherous smiles, or white-haired boys and girls with pale blue eyes that looked like ice. As they got closer, I saw that when they grinned, their teeth were as sharp as razors. Amarjeet rang the bell and the fairies fell back, fading into shadows and melting behind the trees again.

A few of the little kids were crying, and all of them were whimpering, "I'm cold ... I'm hungry ... I want to go home."

"It's not so bad here," Sookie said rather impatiently. "But if you're that miserable, we'll take you back home as soon as we can." That's when my sister spotted me. She shrugged her shoulders and shook her head. "These kids don't like it here."

"Where's Skeeter?" Clive shouted.

"Oh, Skeeter doesn't mind it here. He wants to stay and play some more," Sookie said matter of factly. "Jasper's exasperated," she sighed.

Only my sister would use a word like that at a time like this.

"What do you mean?" I asked calmly, desperate to know more about my friend.

"Jasper's mad because he can't make Skeeter come with us. But he doesn't understand. Skeeter and I still have to find Buddy."

"A little help here!" cried Amarjeet. "I've been ringing this bell for so long my arm's going to fall off." She lowered her voice and said, "Can we leave now?"

"What about Skeeter?" asked Clive. "We're not going without him."

"Help us get the kids back into the tunnel, and I'll come back to get him," I promised.

"Me too," said Sookie.

Right, like that might happen, I thought. Mia, Clive, and I flanked the circle of children, brandishing holly branches and keeping the wraith-like fairies at bay while we backed up all the way to the tunnel.

We almost made it.

Standing in front of the tunnel entrance were my old soccer coaches, Ms. Sinster and Ms. Maliss.

"Hello, Cat," said Ms. Sinster. Her long black hair hung like a veil over her head, and her eyes, still grey as gravestones, bore into me.

Sookie pushed up to the front of our group and was about to walk right past the deadly coaches. But I grabbed her arm and held her back.

"These kids want to go home now," Sookie calmly told the coaches, as if they were teachers or neighbors and not evil-looking sorceresses. "I think you should allow them."

The coaches shook their heads, and Ms. Maliss tucked a long white strand of hair behind her pointed ear. "Sorry, Sookie dear." She actually said that with some affection, but it turned my stomach upside down all the same. "Don't you remember? Father Winter is going to need the children's blood to keep the solstice going for centuries. We require one drop of blood from each child – blood drawn by the holly leaf."

"Take my blood," I said suddenly

Ms. Maliss grinned, and it reminded me of the type of sly nasty gash in a jack-o'-lantern's mouth. Mia wasn't completely correct. Fairies did have beautiful features, but their smiles were ugly.

"I don't think that's a good idea," Sookie whispered to me. "The fairies don't like you much."

"Here," I held out my fingers. "Take ten drops of blood from me. Let the children go, and let Jasper and Skeeter leave. Okay?"

With a wicked grin Ms. Maliss said, "Did I forget to mention that holly leaves in Fairy are poisonous? It could be deadly if you have to prick your hand ten times. But possibly not ..." She laughed. It sounded like a witch's cackle.

Several of the children began to cry louder. I was actually relieved when I saw that my sister began to look alarmed. Fairy hadn't completely enchanted her – she still cared about others.

Both Ms. Sinster and Ms. Maliss rubbed their long slender fingers together. "A fairy fighter's blood is powerful," said Ms. Sinster. "A deal like that is hard to resist."

"Don't, Cat," Sookie begged.

"You can't trust them," Amarjeet said through gritted teeth.

Not at all, I thought, because fairies were tricksters. But maybe I had my own trick planned. As Ms. Maliss and Ms. Sinster parted and stood on each side of the tunnel, I shoved Amarjeet forward and whispered that she shouldn't worry about me because she and Mia had to get the children out of Fairy.

"You climb the stairs backward," I told Mia, "and take your flashlight and my flashlight and shine the lights back down the tunnel. Celts used light on the solstice to keep fairies at a distance."

Mia nodded and ushered her sister and the other kids into the tunnel.

"Hurry, you two," I said to Clive and Sookie.

"I'm not letting you do this." Sookie got that stubborn look. "I'll stay – the fairies won't hurt me. Besides, Skeeter and I have to – " before my sister could finish, I took out my white feather and put it in her hand.

Sookie stared at the white feather she clutched in her hand as it glowed blue, green, and silver. A guilty frown tugged at her mouth. "But Mom said I could go up the hill. I didn't sneak away, I asked permission ..."

A tear trailed down Sookie's cheek, and I quickly tucked the feather in her pocket before the coaches noticed.

"You know something wasn't right with Mom," I said.

Sookie hung her head.

"I need you to go now ... in case it takes me a little while ..." I tried to keep my voice level. "It's really cold in our house, Sookie. Mom's going to need more blankets."

Then I whispered something in my sister's ear. Slowly Sookie nodded and gave me a hug. "Don't forget Buddy," she said. Then she joined the other children.

"What did you say to your sister?" Clive asked me.

"Just that magic is misdirection. Don't worry – I'll get your brother."

"And I've got your back," said Clive, refusing to leave.

Mia, Amarjeet, and Sookie led the children away, as Clive and I remained behind with Ms. Maliss and Ms. Sinster. As soon as the last person disappeared into the tunnel, the fairy children spilled from the trees.

"We made a deal," I reminded my former coaches.

"We did," said Ms. Maliss, pointing to herself and Ms. Sinster. "But I can't account for the rest of the fairies." A Grimoire girl and a white-haired boy rushed into the tunnel, but they screamed and came flying back inside, rubbing their eyes. Mia hadn't waited before she turned on the flashlight.

"No matter," said Ms. Sinster. "We'll have Cat's blood."

I tried ignoring my pounding heart as Clive and I followed the coaches and the fairy children back into the clearing.

CHAPTER 27

A Tithe of Blood

I STARED AT the holly bush with its shiny green leaves that had nasty pointed edges, and I wondered just how poisonous it was – in case my plan didn't work.

"We're in a rush," Ms. Sinster said to me brusquely. "Hold out your hand and when we cut you, let the blood drip in a circle around the holly bush."

"First I need to see Jasper and Skeeter," I said.

"Who said that was part of the deal?" Ms. Maliss replied with a sly smile.

Clive stood beside me and surprised me by putting his arm around me. "We're not moving until we have my brother and our friend."

When did we end up on the same team? I wondered.

Ms. Sinster clapped her hands and two Grimoire girls scurried into the trees. As we waited, the red sky began to darken into a deeper crimson glow. A wisp of orange cloud cast a shadow on the white moon, giving it the appearance of a skull. A horrible chill made my teeth chatter. My scarf, coat, and hat didn't help at all because the cold was coming from inside me.

"We need your blood now," Ms. Maliss insisted. A few of the fairy children began moaning and fading into the darkening shadows. Ms. Maliss seemed to float toward me, her long black dress trailing like a tattered web along the snowy ground. The fairies were losing their grip on the enchantment. Like the moon, their power was waning as the solstice passed. If only I could stall a bit longer ...

"Blood," Ms. Maliss reached for my arm. I snatched it away.

"Fine, but I will do it myself," I said as bravely as I could.

"Cat, Sookie was right," Clive urged. "This is a bad idea."

Then I did something I found terrible and so hard to do in front of Clive. I pretended to weep. "I ... I'm so afraid ..." And then I made dramatic sobbing sounds.

"Don't do it," said Clive.

I have to admit I was touched by the care in his voice, even though I hated acting weak in front of him. "Take half my blood too," Clive told the fairies. "Maybe that way we won't get too much poison," he then whispered to me. But Ms. Maliss only laughed. Several fairies emerged from the trees and grabbed Clive and held him back.

I continued my fake-crying as I stood near the bush. One thing I learned in soccer is that you can't always be the star, not if you want to win. As the saying goes, sometimes you have to take one for the team. I had to act terrified if I was going to convince the fairies that I was cutting my fingers on poisoned leaves and sacrificing my blood to them. The more it looked as if I was suffering, the more those wicked creatures would be distracted.

Ms. Sinster and Ms. Maliss held Clive back as two Grimoire girls half-dragged me to the holly bush.

Then as soon as the girls let me go, I slashed a holly leaf across my finger and made an agonized scream as a drop of blood landed on the white snow. Or at least, that's what I made it look like. When I told Sookie how magic was misdirection, I meant that human magic was supposed to be about cleverness and creating an illusion.

When we'd been helping the children into the tunnel, no one had noticed me reaching into my backpack, and stuffing into my pockets the rowan berries I'd brought. Forenza had said rowan was a powerful agent for fighting fairies. Then when Clive stood in front of me, trying to defend me, I slipped the berries into my hands.

So instead of actually cutting my finger, I only grazed it with the prickly leaf. I dropped a rowan berry from my hand onto the snowy ground so that it looked like a drop of my blood. By the time I dropped the sixth red rowan berry onto the snow and cried out, I heard Jasper.

"Stop, Cat – please."

I looked up and saw that the fairies had brought Skeeter and Jasper into the clearing. They stood beside Clive, and all the boys looked horrified by my fake suffering. My face burned for tricking them too, but I kept on going.

When I dropped the tenth berry, I stumbled toward my friends and drew my hand across my face, pretending to wipe my tears. I sniffled before I said in a broken voice, "Can we go now?"

The fairies' laughter shattered like glass, and they began closing in on us. Then the sky grew dark as the burning embers of a dying fire and the moon began to sink into the horizon. A warmer gust of wind blew into the clearing, and the fairies began to withdraw from us, howling as they were forced back into the trees' shadows.

Ms. Sinster shrieked, "You wretched child. What have you done? The blood tithe didn't work." Then she screamed even louder, "The night is almost over and the solstice is passing!"

Ms. Maliss and Ms. Sinster appeared to leap toward me, but even though Clive and Jasper hurried to my side, it didn't matter. A strong wind began blowing Ms. Maliss and Sinster back into the shadows.

"You'll regret this," screeched Ms. Maliss. "Sookie's friend – Father Winter – is the Holly King, a most powerful fairy lord. He will never let you leave Fairy."

A feeling of doom suffocated me, and an urgent voice in my head said, "Now you've done it."

The other kids and I took off in a full sprint.

Just as we were about to head into the tunnel, we passed another holly tree much larger than the bush in the clearing. I let out a sharp cry, and this time I wasn't faking. I looked at the back of my hand and a deep scratch stretched across it, down to the tip of my index finger. Blood welled along the scratch, and my hand began to burn.

A holly branch from the tree beside the tunnel had actually reached out and grabbed me.

CHAPTER 28

A Deadly Clash

TURNING AROUND, I watched in horror as the leaves and branches on the tree shifted, spilling the snow from their treacherous leaves as they reached out toward me. Then the leaves of the tree grew even larger and more terrifying. It was like looking into a diabolical kaleidoscope – the leaves twisted and turned until they settled into the shape of a giant holly man who towered above me.

"My tithe," a voice boomed so loud that my ears ached and the last of my courage shattered. The holly man took one step toward me, and the leaves that made up his shape quivered as he moved. When he slammed his foot down, the whole ground shook.

"Oh crap," was all I could say.

Clive pushed his brother into the tunnel, and then he raced toward me with Jasper close behind. In a pathetic attempt to defend me, Clive whipped out his own holly branch and brandished it like a sword. Jasper produced his white feather and waved it. Of course Jasper had his feather. He'd been suspecting the fairies were involved when Sookie had made Skeeter disappear. But I wouldn't listen.

For a moment I thought the boys' weapons would help because the green man hesitated.

"Pathetic mortals." The giant holly man's laugh was so cold and evil I started to run, but the mass of green leaves shook and shifted, blocking the tunnel. Then he jolted his terrifying head in my direction, and my knees buckled under me. My legs turned to Jell-O.

Clive dropped the holly branch and fumbled until he pulled his flashlight from his pocket. When he aimed the light at who was surely the Holly King Forenza had mentioned, a few dangerous, sharp leaves wilted back, but the holly man was so huge, there was plenty of him left to do lots of damage. The Holly King blasted us again with an ear-shattering cry. Jasper and I moaned in pain, and Clive dropped his flashlight.

In a desperate attempt to survive, I yanked the bare rowan branch from my pack and began poking it at the oncoming monster. I knew that if I lived, I'd remember his laugh in my nightmares for the rest of my life.

The towering, hideous creature lurched forward as we cowered.

A dark shadow fell over us and across the snow in the shape of some gigantic prehistoric bird. The Holly King bellowed, but this time in an agonizing scream. Clive, Jasper, and I collapsed to the ground and covered our ears.

The air twisted around our bodies strong enough to lift us a foot off the ground. We were caught in the middle of a tornado.

"Grab onto something," I cried out, and I took hold of a black branch as the wind tore away its silver leaves. Clive and Jasper held on to the branch above mine, and I had to duck their kicking feet.

Leaves flew as if someone was taking a chainsaw to a holly tree, and more howls sliced open the air. The giant shadow wings of the sky creature flapped and thundered.

There was another blast of air, only this time it was warm. I smelled cherry blossoms and lilac and briefly wondered if this was what it was like to die – that you remember something pleasant in your last moment.

The holly man seemed to grow even larger, but this time there were spaces between his leaves and branches. Then in another ear-splitting clap, all his leaves blew apart and scattered around us as we covered our heads.

When the last leaf seemed to settle, we let go of the branches and slipped to the ground. As I stood up, a robin flew past me and landed on a black branch above my head, the one that Jasper and Clive had just dropped from. The bird's chest moved in and out rapidly, and its feathers were mussed as if he'd just been in a fight with a cat and had barely escaped. He cocked his head my way and let out a weary chirp. I must have been delusional by this time because it almost seemed as if the little bird had told me to run for it.

Muddled thoughts moved sluggishly through my brain as I wondered what had happened to the giant pterodactyl that should be scooping us up and tearing us to pieces right about now. I felt someone tug me forward and I dimly noticed Jasper dragging me into the tunnel. Clive and Skeeter were just ahead and were already on the first steps of the staircase.

Even as we raced up the stairs, I could hear the clamor of footsteps behind us. I'd given my flashlight to Mia, and Clive had dropped his on the ground so there was no light to hold back the fairies. We ran even faster. As we neared the top of the stone staircase inside the dark tunnel, we began to sputter and choke as smoke billowed toward us. Coughing, we burst through the doorway onto the human side of Grim Hill.

"Are you trying to smother us?" gasped Jasper.

Mitch, who'd been fanning the fire with branches of

holly leaves, paused, his branch hovering near the flame of the Yule log. "We were only following orders."

"And don't stop," I managed to choke out as we heard a treacherous clamor of angry shouts behind us. I grabbed a handful of ivy and threw it on the fire. "Where are the other kids?" I asked frantically, looking for my sister.

"Mia and Amarjeet took them down the hill," said Zach. "They'll be tucked in their beds when their parents begin to come out of the spell." He looked at the stairwell. "I hope we make it back to our beds," he gulped.

"Come on – hurry – build up the flames," I cried to the others.

Zach and Emily joined Mitch and fanned the Yule logs, while Jasper and I grabbed more holly and ivy and threw it all on the fire. Tons of red glowing eyes winked back at us from the entrance of the staircase.

"Shine the flashlights!" I shouted. Mitch, Zach, and Emily turned the flashlights on and aimed them at the tunnel. Screams echoed up from the underground passage. Jasper and Clive grabbed a flaming branch and waved it in front of the tunnel. Skeeter was about to do the same, but I grabbed the burning branch from him.

The deep purple sky began to lighten at the edge of the horizon. It was dawn and the solstice had passed. I'd forgotten how time moved differently between Fairy and our world. Then with an eerie creak, the door began to slam shut as white hands and long curling fingers reached from within the passage trying to hold the door open.

The hill began shaking and we were forced back from the entrance while rocks began shifting and moving on the ground, bouncing around as if we were in the middle of an earthquake. We all ran from the rubble until the shaking stopped.

When it seemed safe, we moved through the crushed rock and brick and looked for the doorway into Fairy.

But all we could see was a pile of dirt.

CHAPTER 29

The Secrets Deepen

THE PORTAL TO Fairy had disappeared, so now there was no way back.

Or so I hoped.

"We'd better get down the hill and into our houses before the town wakes up," I said, feeling more tired than I ever had in my life.

As we trudged down the hill, my head ached and my stomach cramped. The last time I'd had anything to eat was breakfast, and now it was almost dawn the next day. You didn't notice the hours and minutes passing in fairy time, but it still wore you out – it was as if you'd just played a three-day soccer tournament. I reached down and grabbed a handful of snow and shoved it in my mouth. The cold water dripping down my throat helped my terrible thirst. Then I took some more snow and rubbed it on the holly scratch along my hand, which eased the burning a little.

Everyone else, though, acted a lot more energetic. Skeeter was babbling something about how he had such an "awesome time" and couldn't wait to go back there to "play." Zach, Mitch, and Emily kept doing high-fives and were calling themselves "fairy fighters."

Didn't they realize how close we had come to total disaster?

Clive ran up from behind and began walking beside me.

"Don't worry," he whispered. "I won't ever tell how

scared you got – and that you started crying. I was scared too.
But guys don't cry."

"Wait a minute," I said, "that was only an illusion – I
had to fake ..."

Then Clive patted me on the shoulder. "I said I'd never
tell." Then he joined Mitch and Zach and shared his own
Fairy battle tales.

I wanted to argue with him, but finally I realized it just
wasn't worth it. For one thing, lots of people cried – girls and
guys. If Clive couldn't figure that out, it wasn't my problem.
And if he thought I was really sobbing, I guess I could live
with that too – especially when I heard Jasper laughing
behind me.

"Next time," Jasper said, "maybe you'll listen to me
when I say something's just not right."

"And maybe you're starting to understand what it's like
trying to deal with Clive," I muttered.

"Oh, let me see," said Jasper. "Can I understand what it
is like trying to deal with someone who is smart, brave,
insanely focused, fiercely protective of a younger sibling, and
confident to the point of being pig-headed ... does that sound
like anyone else you know, Cat?"

I didn't bother answering, but I couldn't stop the smile
that began to spread across my face. I hadn't smiled in a long
time – maybe not since the last time Jasper and I had argued.

As we got closer to my backyard, Sookie flew from the
house and ran toward me, trudging through the snow in
her blue housecoat and fuzzy slippers. She squealed in relief
and hugged me. Then she smiled at Jasper and grabbed
Skeeter's hand.

"Father Winter has gone to sleep," Sookie announced
approvingly. "I don't hear him anymore." But then a slight

frown tugged her lips, and looking up at me, she said, "He was furious with you, Cat."

"Oh well, he's sleeping now," I said, though even mentioning the Holly King made my hand burn again.

"Where's Buddy?" asked Sookie.

Buddy – oh no.

Sookie's hamster had completely slipped my mind! And now there was no possible way of getting him back.

"I don't see him – where is he?" Sookie asked again as she beamed up at me in an annoying, trusting way. Guilt turned my stomach inside out. Oh crap, little Buddy ... Sookie was going to be so –

"Here he is!" With a grin, Skeeter produced Buddy from a pocket inside his coat. The hamster peeked out from Skeeter's thick mitten, twitched his nose, and leaped onto Sookie's shoulder. She squealed with glee and tried kissing the animal's tiny face.

I breathed a huge sigh of relief, thinking I owed Skeeter big time.

"You did it, Cat – you are the real Queen of Mystery." My sister looked up at me, beaming.

"What do you mean?" I shook my head in confusion.

"Remember how you once told me you had no special talent, I mean, besides soccer? Well, you are the queen of solving mysteries."

I just hoped I could live up to Sookie's admiration. Exhausted, I said, "Let's get you back inside."

The dawn was crisp and cold, but already the thick clouds were breaking up and scudding across the sky. It felt just a bit warmer, but not warm enough for my sister to be standing out in the snow in only a nightgown and a housecoat. "We should help Mom get into bed."

"How are we going to explain all this to my gran?" asked Clive, shaking his head.

"My guess is you won't have to explain anything," said Jasper. "None of us will, especially if you let me bring Skeeter back to the hospital with me. We'll all end up exactly where we're supposed to be."

"Shouldn't we tell the adults the ... the truth?" asked Clive. "Is it right to keep all that's happened secret?"

"No one would ever believe you," Emily said. She shook her head. "I tried telling my parents about Grim Hill after Halloween, and trust me, if you don't want your family giving you weird stares for a few days and whispering to each other as you walk by, just let it go. Besides, after a week, you're not going to be so sure anything strange really did happen."

"That's right," I agreed. "Most likely, today there will be some excuse about a horrible storm last night and about people having fever dreams ..." I drifted off. Grown-ups had ways of explaining everything that didn't fit with what they thought the world should be like. "As Emily said, memories of our creepy experiences just seemed to drift away." Maybe Amarjeet was right – I was getting to be an expert in other-worldly encounters.

"I don't think I'll forget," said Clive. "And I'm pretty sure Skeeter won't."

Sookie and Skeeter were whispering to each other and laughing as if they'd just spent the night at a carnival instead of wrapped up in the fight of our lives. And then my skin prickled as they both began to sing that eerie tune that I'd heard Sookie hum alone in her room while she stared out her window at Grim Hill.

Those other children had been crying and were afraid

when Amarjeet and Mia had taken them out of Fairy – they'd been desperate to go home. That seemed quite sensible to me. But Fairy had a different affect on Sookie and Skeeter – why?

CHAPTER 30

A Grim Return

I SAID GOODBYE to my friends and dragged Sookie away from Skeeter. Every part of me ached, and as I climbed the porch one step at a time, I told Sookie, "I think you need to get a safer hobby – maybe parachuting." She laughed, but I was only half-joking. I'd had enough of the adventurous life, and it felt great to finally crawl into my own soft, warm bed.

Late the next morning, my mother was waking me up. The scent of hot chocolate wafted into my room.

"C'mon, Cat, it's not like you to sleep so late. We've got to go into town and get some Christmas shopping done. Christmas is only a few days away."

I tugged my flannel housecoat on and stumbled down the stairs to the kitchen. Sookie was already up and was crunching her frosty oats. She was almost bouncing off her seat in excitement. "C'mon, Cat, we're getting our tree today! You never sleep later than me – it's already nine-thirty."

I expected my mother to act as if nothing happened last night, but Sookie? However, when the phone rang and my mother went to answer it, Sookie gave me a sly wink. I decided she didn't seem to have as much trouble as I had juggling the magical world and our world. This morning I felt as if I had horrible jet lag and was still recovering from a night of weird dreams.

"Good news," said my mother when she returned to the kitchen. "That was Mia's mom on the phone – she was calling us from the hospital. Jasper and Skeeter are out of the hospital, and everyone is getting better. The flu epidemic is over!" Mom leaned against the counter and admitted, "That terrible bug seemed to skip Sookie, but I was so worried you were coming down with it, Cat."

Skipped Sookie – Mom had that right. But like the last time, Mom seemed to have no recollection of the night that just passed – of her sitting in a chair watching her kid walk out into a blizzard. It wasn't just her though, none of the adults remembered the night before. When I talked to Jasper later that day he said the teachers thought that they'd stayed all night at the school with the children whose parents hadn't been able to make it through the snow to pick them up.

Like I said, adults had a way of rationalizing everything. Still, it ended up being a good holiday. Everyone in town was relieved that the worst of the cold weather was over and that there were no more bizarre temperature fluctuations. While most of the snow melted away, there was enough snow left on the ground for a white Christmas.

This was our first Christmas since my parents' divorce, and I wondered how different it was going to be. We didn't hear from our dad at all. Mom said he was working on a special project, and that he'd get in touch with us when he could. Mom let Sookie and me stay up all night Christmas Eve watching DVDs and playing Christmas music until we both fell asleep on the couch. Christmas morning, Sookie still managed to wake up early – it was the only day of the year she was a morning person. We opened gifts, and I got a cool pair of jeans and a green sweater that actually matched the streaks in my hair. Sookie got a fancy new hamster cage for Buddy that had tunnels and a maze. She and Buddy played with it all day. We invited Jasper and his parents for turkey dinner, and I decided that as long as you could have a bunch of people together on a holiday, it still felt pretty special.

But all good things had to end, and after a week of lazing around, it was time to return to school.

The first morning back, Jasper and I found our friends crowded around my locker. As usual they were talking about soccer.

"Because of the snowstorm, they rescheduled the intra-murals for the third week in January," Mia said to me. "What a lucky break, huh?"

I'd say! And I was glad my friends realized they needed me on their team. So I was surprised when Mia added, "That announcement gave us a chance to make a great decision, Cat."

"What?" I asked, confused. "What am I missing?"

Zach, Mitch, and Clive sauntered over and stood beside us. Clive said "Us, what you're missing is us?"

"Huh?" was all I could say.

"We're going to have a co-ed team," said Emily. "I mean, what a waste when the girls were competing against the boys."

"Exactly," said Zach. "Instead of trying to expose each others' weaknesses, if we play to each others strengths we'll make the gold team – and then we'll be unbeatable."

"Cool!" said Jasper.

But who will get to be the team captain, I wondered. A girl or a guy? The bell rang and I went off to science class with Mia. We had a pop chemistry quiz, and I got 19 out of 20 – a record high. Smiling to myself, and imagining my picture one day up on the giant collage Ms. Dreeble had created of important women scientists, I tossed my textbook in my backpack. Ms. Dreeble called me to her desk.

She looked right at me and sighed. "Cat, that is a good mark you got on your science quiz. But I'm concerned that soccer-wise, it is still so hit-and-miss with you." She drummed her pencil on the desk. "You didn't even show up after school the day of the intramural game – after I explicitly reminded you to be on time."

"But the bus was turned back, and the game was cancelled. So it didn't count."

"Are you a clairvoyant? Can you predict the future and just decide on your own not to show up?" Ms. Dreeble frowned. "I'm sorry, but Mr. Morrows and I have been talking. I admit you have good leadership skills, but you're just not responsible enough. We've decided to make Clive the team captain of the new co-ed team."

Shaking my head, I threw my pack over my shoulder and walked silently to history class, only to see six shocking words written on the board: Hand in your history term paper.

Crap! What paper?

I watched in horror as everyone placed the completed assignment on Mr. Morrows' desk.

I sat down with a thud and put my opened history book in front of my face to avoid Mr. Morrows' stern glance. When Mom saw my history mark, I was going to wind up grounded.

"When did he assign the essay?" I mumbled to no one in particular.

"Last history class before the holiday, when you decided to duck out before the end," said Clive.

"I didn't duck out," I said in an even tone. "If you recall, I was called to the office."

"Right, were you in trouble again?" Clive grinned. When Mitch made those kind of jokes, I thought they were funny. Clive was just plain annoying.

I kept staring at my history book, but for some reason, he kept bugging me.

"Did you hear who the new team captain of the soccer team is going to be?" he asked.

I sighed. Looks as if things were back to normal all right. Once again, as the magic dissolved around the town, I was back to starting from scratch. I'd learned a few things, though. For one, instead of letting Clive bait me, I simply shrugged and said, "Do tell! Who is the new captain?" as if I couldn't care less. By the time I got home, though, I'll admit I was feeling a little low despite knowing that once again, I'd managed to help drive the fairies back into the hill and keep everyone – including myself – safe.

"What's wrong, Cat? Was school all right?" Mom had noticed my quiet mood.

Usually I said that nothing was wrong – that everything was great – but this time I said, "Clive gets on my nerves. Why doesn't he just ignore me if he doesn't like me?"

"Hmm," Mom said. "Sometimes that's a sign."

"A sign for what?" I asked

Mom had that kind of look that parents get when they're in on some big secret – one that only grown-ups can figure out.

I hated that look.

CHAPTER 31

A Cunning Girl

MY MOM HAD been making coffee and she asked me if I'd like some. I was amazed – that was a grown-up offer, and she never let me buy those coffee drinks at the shops. But even though she only poured a tiny bit of coffee in a cup and filled the rest of the mug with hot milk, it was a big treat.

"Café au lait," she said handing me the mug. "It's all the rage in Paris."

I knew she was trying to be funny in her own Mom way. "So what do you mean that Clive's bugging me all the time is a 'sign'?" I asked again.

"You know, a lot of times when a boy gives a girl too much attention, it's because even arguing is better than her not noticing him at all."

I almost spilled my café au lait. No, that couldn't be it. What a dreadful thought that such an arrogant guy could be interested in me. Clive so conceited that he couldn't be hung up on anyone but himself. Could he?

"If that's how he acts when he likes somebody, then I'd hate to get on his bad side," I said sipping my drink.

But then I thought of Zach and how he was so polite to me. Only, he was polite to everyone. Yet if Emily walked in the room, his eyes followed her and no one else. So even though I was sort of interested in Zach, he only noticed Emily, and he wasn't aware that Clive always caught Emily's attention. And Jasper wanted Mia to notice him, but he never saw the admiring glances Amarjeet sent his way. And Mia didn't care about Jasper. She liked Mitch. And come to think of it, even though Emily always tried to get Clive's attention, I was the only girl he talked to at all.

"This is way too complicated," I said. "It's better if I just think about soccer, something I can understand."

The phone rang, but we didn't have to get it as Sookie beat us to it.

"Great news," she screeched interrupting us. "Lucinda and Alice Greystone are back." She handed the phone to Mom, saying to me, "I updated them on the latest calamity. They want to see us."

No kidding, I thought.

"You are welcome to it," I heard Mom say on the phone. "Sookie was just using it to play with."

When Mom got off the phone she said to me, "Sookie offered to lend the Greystone sisters our trunk. They are apparently on a quick stopover from their travels and could really use it. How on Earth did you get to chatting about the trunk?" she asked my sister. "I thought you'd never want to part with it for your magic act."

I wonder if Mom noticed that Sookie looked rather solemn when she shrugged her shoulders and never exactly answered her question.

***

After we picked up the trunk from the school, we pulled up to the Greystone sisters' house, and as soon as Mom turned off the car ignition, Sookie was up the stairs and through their door. That left only me to help with the trunk. The holly scratch on my hand had left a white scar, and I noticed when I handled the trunk my hand began to burn and itch. Before we got to the stairs, Jasper came out and helped carry it. That freed me to run up the steps and give Alice and Lucinda a huge hug.

Lucinda had lost the ghostly pale skin she'd had after spending decades in Fairy. Her face was now tanned, and both she and Alice Greystone sported close-cropped hair. They looked pretty trendy for older ladies.

When Mom drove off, Lucinda held me at arm's length and said, "So our brave fairy fighter has succeeded again!"

Funny, after everything I'd been through, now my eyes began to tear up for real. Good thing Clive wasn't around.

I sniffed, and as I stood in the hallway accepting the lace handkerchief Alice had offered me, I told Lucinda and Alice Greystone about the terrible battle. "What I don't understand is that it seemed as though a robin had defeated the Holly King. The robin was a tiny bird, but when it flew over us, its shadow was as big as a pterodactyl."

"Fairies are a warring bunch," said Lucinda. "I fear you stumbled into an ancient conflict between the Holly King – the father of winter – and the Oak King – the lord of spring." Lucinda looked at the scar on my hand. "You've made a powerful enemy of the Holly King. And when you fed the robin your slice of bread, you also made an important ally. The robin was the Oak King, lord of spring, and he saved you, Cat."

"Well, that's a good thing, isn't it?"

Lucinda patted my arm. "I'm afraid that with fairies, it is better not to be noticed at all."

Too late for that, I thought. Lucinda and Alice brought me into their parlor, which was now restored to pristine condition. All Forenza's books and artifacts had been removed, and I could smell lemon oil after a thorough dusting.

Jasper finished dragging the trunk inside, and he and Alice Greystone took it downstairs to their cellar.

"I hope you don't mind the white lie I told your mother about us needing the trunk for our travels," said Lucinda. "But I wanted to make sure we could store this safely. As you found out, magical items can be quite hazardous. Especially if they land in the wrong hands," she said glancing at Sookie.

"Why not just get rid of the trunk altogether?" I asked.

Shaking her head, Lucinda said, "Bad idea. Fairy objects have a way of turning up again in all the wrong places."

Like the trunk turning up in our attic, I thought. Then I began to wonder whom the trunk actually belonged to, and I was going to ask Lucinda if she had any idea, when Alice and Jasper came back upstairs.

"Got it tucked away safely," said Alice. "Do I hear the kettle boiling?"

Lucinda went into the kitchen with Sookie, and she returned with a steaming pot of tea. Jasper rolled his eyes at my sister, who was following behind Lucinda. I held my breath as I watched Sookie teeter with a plate of oatmeal cookies in one hand and a tray of cups and saucers that tipped precariously in the other hand. I knew full well she'd insisted on helping. I hurried to grab the edge of the tray and I made sure everything was delivered in one piece onto the gleaming and freshly polished coffee table.

"Isn't Forenza staying here anymore?" I asked.

"She cleared out fast," Alice Greystone sighed. "She found this place very unsettling."

"Imagine," said Lucinda, "spending all those years studying fairy lore and Celtic mythology, and not recognizing fairies were practically tapping on her window."

"Oh, I think she recognized it," I said. "I'm sure that was the 'unsettling' bit."

Lucinda and Alice couldn't quite cover up their smiles. Then they each went to the bookcase and carried back three small narrow boxes wrapped in red tissue paper with big green bows.

"A belated Christmas gift from us," said Alice Greystone.

We thanked them and then tore open the gifts. Jasper held up a finely tooled leather belt carved with what Lucinda said were "Celtic runes." The belt had a small scabbard attached. Sookie and I had belts of a fine and delicate silver rope, with three tiny Celtic charms. There was a small clip on each belt.

"Attach your white feathers to your belts," said Lucinda. "Don't decide to put your feather in a safe place and then forget about it," she said looking at me. "Or," Lucinda said gazing fiercely at Sookie, "don't stuff your white feather in your sock drawer when you find a new feather you like better."

I didn't like how guilty Sookie looked when Lucinda had said that last part.

"Do you have something for me, Sookie?" Lucinda asked. "A turban with a black feather, perhaps?"

Reluctantly, Sookie stood up and said, "It's in my backpack." When Sookie left the room, it was a good time to ask something that had been bothering me ever since I'd returned from Grim Hill.

"When we went into Fairy to rescue the children, they were all crying and scared – except for Sookie and Skeeter. The only reason I think they even left Fairy is because Clive and I made them leave."

"They are cunning children," said Lucinda.

"If you mean Sookie's crafty and smart, I agree, but I still don't understand."

"I mean, when children are in Fairy they can react in two ways," explained Lucinda. "They can pine away in misery, or they can thrive because there was already magic inside them. There have always been certain children who are sensitive to what most of us cannot see."

That did sound like Sookie. "So what do I do? I'm afraid she'll start messing with magic again. She and her new friend Skeeter sing strange songs and act as if they are in on some deep secret."

"I'm sure they are," said Lucinda. "And I think if we try to separate your sister from the magical world, she'll hide it from us and will be vulnerable to other influences."

"I knew it," muttered Jasper.

"Better she learns to develop magic wisely," said Lucinda. Then Sookie came in carrying her purple turban with the black feather.

"I'll pack this away with the trunk," said Lucinda, taking the turban away from the Queen of Mystery, who I now realized was very mysterious indeed.

"Perhaps we can arrange some regular visits where we can monitor Sookie's magic," Alice suggested to Lucinda.

"That sounds way better than piano lessons," Sookie agreed.

"How can I help?" I asked, worrying about what Sookie might get up to next.

"You need to watch over your little sister," said Alice Greystone. "She is precocious, but she is still too young and doesn't always know what she's doing."

"Sometimes I think I'm encouraging her to do one thing

..." I said looking directly at Sookie,"... but it's a whole other thing that she's up to," I continued, thinking back to the talent show.

"Helping Father Winter do wicked things was an accident," complained Sookie

"All of you can be influenced by fairy magic. That's why you should always keep your feathers handy," warned Alice Greystone.

I was beginning to realize that being next to Grim Hill was only one of my problems and that my feather wasn't the only thing I was going to have to keep close.

I was going to have to keep a very close eye on Sookie and her friend Skeeter.

THE END?

From the "Grim Hill" Series

The Secret of Grim Hill

Cat Peters just transferred to Darkmont High and is already
desperate to get out. When she hears that Grimoire,
the private school on the hill, is offering scholarships to
the winners of a Halloween soccer match, Cat jumps at the
chance. Her little sister, Sookie, and their bookworm
neighbor, Jasper, try to tell her there's something ... *just not
right* about the old school, and their worries are confirmed
when they uncover a mystery about an entire soccer team
that disappeared many years ago. Further investigation leads
Cat to a book about ancient Celtic myth and fairy lore, and
she soon realizes that there is something truly wicked at
work inside the walls of Grimoire.

www.grimhill.com

The Uncle Duncle Chronicles:
Escape from Treasure Island
by Darren Krill / 978-1-897073-31-5

Sage Smiley is going on vacation with his favorite uncle, world famous explorer Dunkirk Smiley (a.k.a. "Uncle Duncle"), using the powers of a magical talisman to go wherever he wants. But the aerial adventure goes awry when Sage's imagination brings them to Robert Louis Stevenson's *Treasure Island*. Together they must free a group of prisoners from the clutches of Long John Silver, lay claim to the glittering chests of pirate treasure, and fight for their very lives.

"... the next best thing to a sequel [to **Treasure Island**] ..."
– *Quill & Quire*

"Non-stop fun and action ..."
– *CM: Canadian Review of Materials*

"It's a rollicking adventure ... custom-made to spark the imagination ..." – *Edmonton Sun*

www.lobsterpress.com

Stolen Voices

by Ellen Dee Davidson / **978-1-897073-16-2**

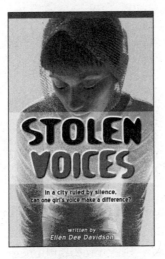

Life in Noveskina is designed to be harmonious and conflict free. But Miri, daughter of two of the city's Important Officials, faces a shameful dilemma. She has matured with no clear Talent and thus faces life among the lower classes. As Miri is confronted with the dark secrets of Noveskina, the quiet peace of her once-perfect world reveals itself as something infinitely more sinister.

"... definitely a page-turner that will keep readers captivated from the start." – *School Library Journal*

"Set in an intriguing fantasy world, Davidson tells a compelling story that will strike a chord with many readers ..."
– Pamela F. Service, author of *The Reluctant God*

Nominated, American Library Association Amelia Bloomer Project (2006)

Selected, International Youth Library's White Ravens Catalogue, An Annual Selection of International Children's and Youth Literature

www.lobsterpress.com

ABOUT THE AUTHOR:

Linda DeMeulemeester has worked in the fields of literacy and education for many years as a teacher and program adviser. She credits her grandmother, a natural storyteller who was born over a hundred years ago, for her love of mystery and suspense. Linda's short stories have been published in several magazines; *The Secret of Grim Hill* was her first novel.